A Summer in São Paulo

These medics are leaving their hearts in South America!

Invited to spend the summer in the high-tech, high-stakes world of São Paulo's premiere teaching hospital, Hospital Universitário Paulista, it's the chance for three visiting medical professionals to shake off their everyday routine—and embrace the vivacity of South America!

While they're certainly turning up the heat during the long working days, the warm days and sultry nights are the perfect setting for romance… And none of them can resist the call of passion in paradise!

Awakened by Her Brooding Brazilian by Ann McIntosh

Falling for the Single Dad Surgeon by Charlotte Hawkes

One Hot Night with Dr. Cardoza by Tina Beckett

All available now!

Dear Reader,

I have been thinking a lot about the past lately. How do we deal with it? Do we ignore it and pretend it never happened? Do we stare back at it and forget to live in the present? Or does the answer lie somewhere in the middle?

Thank you for joining Roque and Amy as they struggle to figure out what to do with their past triumphs and failures. And maybe, just maybe, they'll find a little something extra along their journey—something neither of them expects.

I hope you enjoy reading their story as much as I loved writing it.

Love,

Tina Beckett

ONE HOT NIGHT WITH DR. CARDOZA

TINA BECKETT

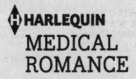

HARLEQUIN
MEDICAL
ROMANCE

HARLEQUIN®
**MEDICAL
ROMANCE™**

Recycling programs
for this product may
not exist in your area.

ISBN-13: 978-1-335-14945-9

One Hot Night with Dr. Cardoza

Copyright © 2020 by Tina Beckett

All rights reserved. No part of this book may be used or reproduced in
any manner whatsoever without written permission except in the case of
brief quotations embodied in critical articles and reviews.

This is a work of fiction. Names, characters, places and incidents
are either the product of the author's imagination or are used fictitiously.
Any resemblance to actual persons, living or dead, businesses,
companies, events or locales is entirely coincidental.

This edition published by arrangement with Harlequin Books S.A.

For questions and comments about the quality of this book,
please contact us at CustomerService@Harlequin.com.

Harlequin Enterprises ULC
22 Adelaide St. West, 40th Floor
Toronto, Ontario M5H 4E3, Canada
www.Harlequin.com

Printed in U.S.A.

Three-time Golden Heart® Award finalist **Tina Beckett** learned to pack her suitcases almost before she learned to read. Born to a military family, she has lived in the United States, Puerto Rico, Portugal and Brazil. In addition to traveling, Tina loves to cuddle with her pug, Alex, spend time with her family and hit the trails on her horse. Learn more about Tina from her website or "friend" her on Facebook.

Books by Tina Beckett

Harlequin Medical Romance

London Hospital Midwives
Miracle Baby for the Midwife

Hope Children's Hospital
The Billionaire's Christmas Wish

Hot Brazilian Docs!

To Play with Fire
The Dangers of Dating Dr. Carvalho
The Doctor's Forbidden Temptation
From Passion to Pregnancy

One Night to Change Their Lives
The Surgeon's Surprise Baby
A Family to Heal His Heart
A Christmas Kiss with Her Ex-Army Doc

Visit the Author Profile page
at Harlequin.com for more titles.

To John, as always.

**Praise for
Tina Beckett**

"Every medical romance I've read by Ms. Beckett
has entertained me from start to finish, as she
writes complex characters with interesting back
stories, compelling dialogue that has me enjoying
the growing relationship between the two main
characters, and challenging obstacles for the
characters to overcome and this story was no
different."

—*Harlequin Junkie* on
One Night to Change Their Lives

CHAPTER ONE

AMY WOODELL ADJUSTED the single strap of her teal gown one last time as she entered the swanky hotel. She'd ripped out the stitches and resewn it in an attempt to pull up the hemline just a bit. But it hadn't quite solved the problem.

In her rush to pack for her trip to Brazil, she'd brought the wrong shoes. The heels on her silver slingbacks were about an inch shorter than the black stilettos she normally would have worn. But she'd been a last-minute addition to the people who'd be attending the summer lecture program at the fabulous Hospital Universitário Paulista. And between a rushed itinerary followed by flight delays, there'd been no time to go shopping. She'd added a silver-linked belt to her waistline as an additional way to keep her dress from dragging the floor.

Glancing through the palm trees and lush tropical decor, she spotted a familiar face in the crowd. Krysta, wasn't that her name? The customs and immigration line had been long, but fortunately she'd met Krysta, who was also part of the group of visiting doctors—a specialist in otolaryngology and facial reconstruction. They'd hit it off almost immediately, the other woman's friendly nature helping put her nerves at ease.

Amy's mom's sudden death six months ago had put her life into a tailspin, making her realize how little firsthand knowledge she'd had about her mother's heritage. Being in Brazil—her mom's home country—made her feel connected to her in a way that defied logic. And she had an uncle she'd never even met, who supposedly lived on the outskirts of São Paulo, according to an address in her mom's things.

Well, she was going to make the most of these three months! And if she could adopt a little bit of her mother's philosophy of living in the moment, even better.

Heading toward Krysta and hoping against hope that the other woman remembered her from the immigration line, she surveyed the room. Round tables were topped with silk damask tablecloths and huge flower-strewn topiaries. The colors and lush tropical theme were like something out of a pricey travel magazine. It was gorgeous.

So were the people.

And Amy had never felt more out of place.

Her eyes met those of a man across the room, his lean physique and good looks making her steps falter for a minute. He stood straight and tall, his black hair melding with his equally black clothing; everything from his suit to his tie to the tips of his polished shoes were dark.

She shivered. He could have been the angel of death or a grim reaper—albeit a gorgeous one—here to mete out swift justice. All he lacked was a scythe. He did have something in his hand, although she couldn't quite tell what it... When she realized she was rooted in place...and that she was staring—*staring!*—she forced her feet back into motion.

Oh, Lord.

Maybe he hadn't noticed. She chanced another quick peek and was thankful to see him talking to some cute blonde, his mouth curving to reveal a flash of white teeth. Her insides gave a deep shiver.

Probably his wife, Amy.

Who thankfully hadn't noticed a strange woman ogling her husband.

She made it to Krysta and forced a smile, although she was suddenly feeling even less sure of her place here. And her reaction to a complete stranger? Ridiculous.

Although if she had been her vibrant, larger than life mother, she would have marched right over and introduced herself to him. Laughed at his jokes. Fluttered her lashes at him a time or two. Cecília Rodrigo Woodell had never met a stranger. Something that used to embarrass Amy. But not anymore.

"Wow, this is quite a welcoming party. I don't know if you remember me. Amy Woodell?"

Krysta nodded. "Of course I do. You're a physical therapist, right?" She got the attention of the woman next to her. "Amy, this is Flávia Maura. She actually works in the Atlantic Forest with venomous snakes and spiders. She's here to give a lecture."

"Nice to meet you. I hate to admit it, but snakes kind of terrify me." She held up her palm, where two small scars were still visible. "Pygmy rattlers are pretty common in Florida. So are pools. And the two of them seem to find each other. A lot."

Flávia shifted her attention from something in the crowd back to Amy and Krysta, smoothing her palms down the front of her dress as if suddenly ill at ease in it.

"Yes, I'm familiar with rattlesnakes. But I'll admit the only snakes that disgust me are the ones that strut around on two legs, brag about their *avô*'s contributions to this hospital and spend much of their time insulting others."

She sent a glare back into the crowd. "But that's neither here nor there. And hopefully neither of you will have to deal with that particular *cobra*." The bits and pieces of Portuguese mixed with her English made the statement sound slightly sinister.

The image of Tall, Dark and Reaperish popped up in her head. Was Flávia talking about him? She'd kind of been looking off in that general direction. If so, Amy should be doubly glad she wouldn't have to work with him. Or flutter her lashes at him.

Although that smile hadn't made him look like a snake. Or even a jerk. But then again, looks could be deceiving. As she'd found out from her job. And her last boyfriend, who'd appeared to be totally into her. Until he wasn't. She'd learned the hard way that "ghosting" was actually a real phenomenon.

From now on she was going to keep things between her and men light and simple. Maybe somewhere in the neighborhood of "fling" territory. And the Reaper? That glance he'd given her had been anything but light or simple.

Flávia smiled. "I see movement by the podium. I think they're getting ready to give the welcomes. *Até logo.*"

"Nice to meet you, Flávia." Amy smiled back before turning to Krysta. "See you soon, too, I hope," she said with a light touch of Krysta's arm. She then began to circle the tables, waiting for further instructions. She almost tripped over the hem of her dress before yanking it up again. Ugh!

The wait was longer than she expected it to be, but just as she was trying to decide whether or not to find Krysta again, someone at the front of the room tapped the microphone. "We want to take a moment to welcome our visiting doctors and lecturers. We're very excited about this year's summer lecture program."

She shifted her weight. She wasn't a doctor. Furthering her education had been on the back burner for a long time, but recently she'd started giving it serious thought and had included that fact on her application.

The speaker's English was excellent. Since there were people here from all over the world, it made sense that they'd address the group in that language. Despite having a mother who was Brazilian, Amy unfortunately hadn't taken advantage of practicing her Portuguese. So, she'd pretty much stuck to short simple phrasings since she'd arrived, although she could understand most of what was said.

"If you haven't already done so, please consult the seating chart at the entrance to find your place. Dinner will be served shortly, so if you could take your seats as soon as possible, that would be appreciated."

Amy took a deep breath and headed over to the seating chart just as someone else was getting there. Sensing someone to her left, she turned with a smile to introduce herself. It quickly faded. It was the Reaper. And up close, those flaws she expected to see were nonexistent. Also nonexistent was the blonde he'd been with moments earlier. She forced herself to speak.

"Hello. I'm Amy Woodell."

"Ah, so you are our physical therapist? I have been wondering about you."

The way he said "our" in that gruff, accented English gave the words a sense of intimacy that made her swallow. It served to reinforce her weird initial reaction to him. She forced her lashes to stay put until her eyes burned with the effort.

Stupid, Amy. Probably married. Remember?

"Yes, I guess I am. And am I the only

one?" She slid a thumb under her the strap of her dress, afraid it might slide down.

"You are indeed. I'm Roque Cardoza, the head of orthopedics. We'll be working together, it seems." He glanced at the seating chart. "And sitting together. Shall we go?"

Working? And sitting? Together? Oh, no!

She blinked a couple of times in rapid succession, her composure beginning to crumble as they made their way to the table. He had a cane in his left hand. Had he injured himself? Not that she was going to ask. "It's very nice to meet you. I'm anxious to get started."

Actually, she was anxious to be anywhere but here, suddenly.

"Yes. As am I."

She shivered. It had to be the language that gave everything that smooth seductive air. She could get addicted to listening to him. And the way his eyes remained fastened to her face the whole time he'd addressed her… But not in a creepy way. Not like how she'd sized him up earlier.

Her thumb dipped out from under her strap, almost wishing it *would* slip, just so they could be on equal footing as far as staring went. Her eyes dropped to his ring finger, but it was empty. Not even a hint that one had been recently removed, although that meant nothing. Lots of people chose not to wear their wedding bands. And it didn't look like staff members had brought their significant others to the soiree, since they didn't seem to be paired up that way.

Roque indicated her seat and waited for her to take it before sliding into his own, propping his cane against the table. He hadn't used the cane to walk and there was no orthopedic boot on his foot, and he'd certainly had no problem maneuvering into his chair. In fact, he was...

Nothing. He was nothing. And he definitely wasn't light. Or simple. Her two new requirements in a man.

Time to squash those fling thoughts that kept circling her head like vultures looking for any sign of weakness.

She turned her attention to the person in the seat to her right. The woman was another visiting doctor from London who specialized in sports medicine.

"The doctor you were speaking with also specializes in sports medicine, I hear, so it'll be interesting to hear things from his perspective."

Was he listening?

"Some of my early physical therapy work was at a center specializing in sports injuries. Those are hard, since most athletes need the affected area of the body in order to perform adequately. Sometimes they never completely recover."

"Yes. Sometimes that is the case. No matter how much physical therapy they may receive." The comment came from Roque. So he *was* listening. And his words had a strange, almost angry quality to them.

Anything she might have said in response was halted as dinner plates were brought around to the tables.

She knew this dish. "This looks like shrimp in coconut milk, like my mom used to make."

"Your mother is Brazilian?"

Amy glanced at him. "Yes. I think she called this *camarão no leite de coco*."

"Very good. So you speak Portuguese as well?"

"I understand a lot. But I'm sorry to say I only have survival-skill fluency as far as speaking goes. My tongue gets tripped up."

His fingers came to rest on the table. "If you understand the mechanics, then it's only a matter of practice for the tongue. Soon it remembers exactly how to move."

She gulped as those vultures continued to circle. Everything he said carried a double-edged whammy that made her senses reel. She'd gotten all kinds of sly innuendos while working on male patients over the years. Both married and unmarried. But she wasn't getting those vibes from Roque. At all. He wasn't doing it on purpose.

And yet she found her body reacting to them—to *him!*—and that horrified her.

"I don't think I'll be here long enough to get in that kind of practice." She decided to rope those vultures and jerk them out of the sky. He was one of the first men she'd actually sat down to talk to in Brazil, so it made sense that she might notice him more than she normally would.

After her mom died, she'd realized how much life the woman had exuded. How many chances she'd taken in the living of it, and how little of herself she'd held back. When Amy was a kid, she'd struggled with having a mother who was so open, so friendly. But only now was she wishing she had a little more of her mom's joie de vivre. Fully embracing any and all opportunities. Including in the area of love.

And Roque?

Not one of those opportunities. Especially if he was involved with someone.

And if he wasn't?

She was only here for three months. If she met someone else, someone other than a man she'd be working with, why not have a little fun? And this time, she'd have no expectations. Unlike her last relationship.

Her mom had met Amy's father while he was in Brazil on business. They'd fallen in love instantly. Before they knew it, they were married, and Amy's mom had uprooted herself from everything she'd known to be with the man she loved. He'd died five years later, and her mom had stayed in Florida to be close to his grave. And now she was buried next to him.

Not something Amy could imagine herself doing. Florida was one of the last links she had with her parents. She actually worked at the hospital she'd been born in.

"If the hospital administration finds out that you understand the language, I can guarantee they will use that to their advantage."

"And if they don't know?"

"Vão descobrir, com certeza."

She took a bite of shrimp, the rich luscious flavors rolling around in her mouth. Swallowing, she said, "They won't find out. Not unless you tell them." Too late she realized that he'd spoken to her in Portuguese.

"I think I will not have to tell them... Amy." Her name came out sounding like "Ahh-Mee," all musical and so horrifyingly attractive.

She licked her lips, trying to maintain her grip on what little composure she had left.

He was right. There was no way she could keep her knowledge of the language a secret. But the truth was, she was embarrassed to speak. She hated making mistakes of any kind. And yet Roque's English wasn't perfect, and he was still willing to try in order to be understood. And at a hospital like Paulista he was probably called on to speak English fairly often. "You're right. I'll give myself away, won't I?"

"Yes. Most assuredly."

She smiled at him, feeling silly all of a sudden. What would her mom have done in this situation? She would have tackled that language barrier and conquered it, just like she'd done when she'd married her father. While her mom had always maintained her accent, she'd spoken English very well. "Well, I won't try to hide it, then."

One side of his mouth kicked up. Not quite as big as the smile he'd lavished on the blonde, but it transformed the rugged lines of his face in ways that made warmth pool in her stomach.

She took a deep breath and dug into her food, hoping to take her attention off the man beside her. Just in time, too. Because the next speaker was at the podium giving instructions on how the scheduling would work. She forced herself to listen, since she didn't want to be lost tomorrow, when things got under way. It seemed those who were not giving lectures would shadow a staff member for the first half of their stay in order to learn the ropes. Then they would be given more latitude and allowed to have input in patient care.

That was exciting. From the information she'd seen online, Paulista would rival any hospital she'd visited in the US.

"For those of you who have just arrived, there is an envelope on the table listing who you'll be paired with. There will be two or three visiting medical professionals shadowing the same staff member. Who knows, you might even be sitting at the same table with them."

There were a few chuckles at that comment, but Amy didn't share in the mirth. Her hands suddenly turned to ice, her fork stopping halfway to her mouth.

She spotted the envelope the woman had mentioned. Cream-colored and tipped with gold, it shouldn't look ominous, but it did. Knowing she couldn't simply drop the fork and dive for the list, she forced herself to pop the shrimp into her mouth and chew as the person to Roque's left drew the sheet from the envelope and glanced at it. The man then passed the paper to Roque, while Amy struggled to swallow her food.

The orthopedist didn't even glance at the names. Instead, a muscle in his jaw flickered and one brow edged up, and he handed the sheet to her, eyes meeting hers and lingering.

Oh, God! Why? Her and...the Reaper?

That's why he'd mentioned working together. She hadn't thought he'd meant so closely together. Amy forced herself to look at the paper in her hands...to find her name. But it was all a pretense. And there it was in black and white: Roque Cardoza, Amy Woodell and two other names.

She didn't know how she'd expected this thing to work but had assumed there'd be some kind of short orientation as a group before listening to the various lecturers and participating in treatment as opportunities arose. But to work closely with someone she was already uneasy with? For half of the three-month stint? That was a whole month and a half. Of watching every move the man made.

She passed the sheet to the woman next to her. Why couldn't she be with Flávia and Krysta?

Because they were both lecturing.

The woman she'd spoken to a few minutes earlier smiled. "It looks like I'm in your group, and I've met the other man on the list as well. He's on the far side of the table."

Okay, so at least that was something. "That's great." But there was no conviction in her voice.

The speaker addressed them again. "So once you've finished dinner, find your group and set a meeting time and place for tomorrow, if you would."

Roque leaned over. "Looks like you're stuck with me for a little longer. But don't worry. I won't tell anyone your little secret."

Little secret?

The words made her heart skip a beat. Then another. Had he guessed what he did to her? Her face became a scorching inferno. "I'm not sure what you mean."

"That you understand Portuguese." He frowned. "Is there some other secret I should know about?"

Her shoulders sagged and her strap actually started to slide down her shoulder. She shrugged it back into place.

"No. No other secrets." *Liar.* "And since we both agreed it would be impossible to keep my Portuguese under wraps, I guess it doesn't matter."

Somehow she got through the rest of the meal, which was followed by a luscious crème brûlée for dessert. Then people were getting to their feet, and groups formed all over the room, the sounds of excitement building in the air.

Except the air where she was sitting.

"So here we are." Roque stood, not reaching for his cane.

She scrambled to her feet as well. "Yes, we are."

It's only six weeks, Amy. You can do this.

The sports medicine doctor introduced herself to the group as Lara Smith. And a man with light brown hair came over and shook Roque's hand and then hers. "I am Dr.

Peter Gunderfeld. You must be Dr. Cardoza and Dr. Woodell?"

Everyone in her group was a doctor. Except for her.

"Just Amy, for me." Her uneasiness about her decision to come to Brazil grew. These people were all brilliantly talented in their respective fields, from what she was discovering. Maybe she should have just planned a vacation to the country and skipped the summer lecture program.

"You can call me Peter, then."

"And Lara is fine with me."

"I am Roque."

The pronouncement landed like a hammer, although she was sure he hadn't meant it to.

They went through a few moments of exchanging social pleasantries about where they were from. She already knew Lara was from England. And Peter was from Munich, Germany.

Roque was from Rio de Janeiro, originally. She had noticed a difference in his speech patterns as opposed to her mom's, who was from São Paulo. Many of his *s*'s had the "sh" sound characteristic of the famous city.

"Did you know that the name Florida comes from the Portuguese word meaning 'flowered'?" Roque's mouth curved slightly. She forced her gaze not to dwell.

"I did." This would be a perfect time to ask what his name meant, but that might be a little too personal.

Peter had no problems sharing personal information, however. He was married with a two-year-old daughter.

"It had to have been hard to leave them at home," Lara said.

"Yes. But they're going to meet me here the last week of our stay, and then we'll vacation in Iguaçu Falls."

"Good choice. Foz do Iguaçu is worth the visit." Roque glanced at Amy. "I hope you and Lara added extra time on to your trip as well."

She hadn't really thought about that. She already had her return ticket, in fact. Maybe she should check to see how hard it would be to switch the dates.

"I've been to Brazil several times actually. And no husband or kids to bring," Lara said, smiling at Peter. "So I'm just here for the conference."

Roque hadn't commented on his relationship status, and Amy wasn't about to ask nor share hers. Not only was it not any of her business, she didn't want him thinking that she was interested in him like that.

She wasn't.

Those thoughts about flings and the flutters in her belly were strictly animal survival instincts. Nothing more. If she stuck to work topics, it should be easier to view him as a colleague and not as a person whose speech patterns did crazy things to her libido.

Maybe she did need to hook up with a good-looking man and knock some of this stuff out of her system. It had been ages since she'd had sex.

She wasn't going to number Roque in with the possible candidates for that, though. Her gaze scouted the room, and while she saw several other attractive men, there was no pull toward them.

Well, all that meant was that she wasn't shallow, right?

Hmm…and yet she'd been glued to almost every word that came out of Roque's firm, sexy mouth.

She rolled her eyes.

The man picked that moment to glance at his watch. "I have an early day tomorrow. Do you all know your way to the condominium?"

"Yes. The Fonte Cristalina, right?" Amy had already dropped her luggage off at the apartment building the hospital had put them up in. It wasn't fancy, but it was clean and had a gorgeous view of the city.

"Yes." Roque looked from one to the other. "It's within walking distance of Paulista. But it's better to do that during the day. So, let's meet in the hospital lobby at eight in the morning?" There was a slight furrow between his brows now, though.

"Very good. I must go call my wife," Peter said. "See you tomorrow."

"And I'm meeting a friend for a nightcap," Lara added a second later.

Amy said her goodbyes. Was she the only one feeling lost at sea?

Maybe Roque sensed some of her thoughts

because he stayed where he was. "Would you like me to drop you off at the apartment complex?"

"Oh, no, it's okay. I can catch a cab. There are some out front, I'm sure."

"Very likely." He moved sideways to let someone through, which put him way too close to her for comfort.

Amy took a quick step back, and a sharp tug at her shoulder was followed by a distinct ripping sound. Then things began a slow slide. Straight down. Including her mind.

Oh! Oh, no!

She grabbed at the bodice of her dress just as the shoulder strap flopped uselessly over the top of her hand.

Roque turned…stared at her shoulder, before glancing down at where his foot was planted on her hem. His face turned a dull red.

"*Merde!* I am sorry, Amy. I did not realize."

Her name came rough-edged off his tongue, and she shut her eyes as hot embarrassment rained down on her. She knew she hadn't stitched the strap enough, but hadn't given much thought to it. A huge mistake.

Just like this whole damned trip.

"It's okay, but I'd better find that cab now."

"I will take you home. It's only right."

The thought of running out of the hotel holding up her dress was mortifying, so she decided to accept his offer. "Thank you. Could you stand in front of me for a second, though?"

His head tilted sideways, but he shifted until they were face-to-face, and much, much closer than they had been last time.

Hot flames licked at her innards, and she had a hard time catching her breath. "I—I kind of meant for you to turn the other way. I want to tuck my strap into my dress so it's not as obvious."

This time, his eyes did what she'd wanted them to do earlier. Trailed over her bare shoulder and lower before coming back up to meet her gaze. That muscle in his jaw twitched the way it had when he'd handed her the list of names, but he said,

"Of course," before turning away from her, shielding her from prying eyes.

She quickly shoved the strap into the front of her dress, hoping it didn't cause any awkward bulges, then she clamped her right arm across her chest and picked up her clutch purse. Where were those few lost pounds when you needed them?

"Okay, you can turn around now."

He did, his glance going back to her shoulders, now bereft of any fabric. "I will pay for the damage I caused."

No, he wouldn't. Because the real damage wasn't anything that could be seen with the naked eye.

"It's my fault. I tried to alter the length on my own, when I should have bought higher heels. I'm just glad it happened at the end of the evening rather than at the beginning."

"I know a very good seamstress. It would also be free."

Oh, God! Maybe he really was married. She could picture him trying to explain to some faceless wife how he'd practically stripped one of his charges naked in front of an entire room of doctors.

Well, not naked. But almost. She didn't have a bra on, since the dress had one built into it. "I'm sure that's not—"

"It is my mother. It would take her little time to make it right. She could even arrange for a fitting to adjust the length, if you would like. Her shop is at my parents' home."

Somehow the fact that his mom was the seamstress made her relax. "That would be an awkward conversation, wouldn't it?"

"No. She's come to expect me to be a little more...clumsy than I used to be."

Inadvertently, her glance shifted to the cane. "You're not clumsy. It was an accident."

He was the most elegant, graceful man she'd met in a long time, whatever the reasons for that cane.

"Yes, well, be that as it may, I do insist on making it right."

Amy had a feeling he wasn't going to let it go. "At least ask your mom if she'd mind, first, before just assuming she'll say yes."

"I will. But I know she will not mind." He gave her that slow smile of his. The one that devastated her senses and made it hard to think beyond it. "Let me do this for you, Amy. This one small thing."

It wasn't a small thing. Not to her. But if she tried to keep arguing the point, he was eventually going to realize there was something more behind it. Something that made her wary of him—wary of working on his team for the next three months. Wary of shadowing him for half of those three months.

So all she could do was agree and say a fitting wasn't necessary, and hope that once the dress was returned, she could forget about this incident once and for all. Maybe then she could focus on her real reasons for coming to Brazil. Those had to do with her mom and finding her uncle. And her career, of course.

And none of those things included the man in front of her.

CHAPTER TWO

DAMN, WHAT HAD he done?

The very physical therapist he'd tried to veto having on his team seemed to be a nice person. But she carried an air of fragility that socked him in the gut and made him wish he'd stuck to his guns. But the physical therapy department was running short-staffed at the moment and couldn't spare anyone to participate in the summer lecture program.

And then he had to go and ruin her dress. And when he'd misunderstood and stood face-to-face with her, almost touching, and definitely close enough to...

Close enough to nothing!

This damned leg. Even as the thought went through his head, a phantom pain shot through his thigh. One that had nothing to do with his reaction to her. Or that dress.

He stepped on the gas as the drive to the apartment seemed to take forever, even though it was less than three blocks away. Part of it was due to navigating in heavy traffic. But also because his peripheral vision kept checking the top of her dress to make sure it hadn't crept any farther down. If that happened, he might have to do a major reboot of his sanity. Because as he'd gazed at her in that room full of people, he'd found himself wishing it would. Which was ridiculous. Not to mention unprofessional.

They finally arrived, and Roque pressed the code into the security box at the front of the building, waiting as the heavy garage door swung open to allow his Mercedes to slide past. It closed behind them with a sense of finality, trapping him in the space with her.

He forced himself to say something in hopes she wouldn't guess where his thoughts were straying. "The hospital bought several apartments in this condominium for visiting doctors or VIP patients coming in from other areas of the country. So everyone's staying at the same place."

"That makes sense." Her dress seemed to edge down a millimeter, and his mouth went completely dry.

He found a parking spot. "Would you like me to wait while you take off the dress?"

"Excuse me?"

A flare went off in his head, sending up an alarm that the rest of his body failed to heed. His thoughts about it sliding down were evidently starting to come out in his speech. "I did not mean in the car, of course. I meant in your apartment. You could bring the dress back down to me, unless you prefer to bring it to the hospital."

Yes, the sooner she was out of sight, the sooner he would be able to get that image out of his head. But he was pretty sure it would reappear—along with a few others—the second he went to sleep tonight.

"Oh, of course." She hesitated. "I'd rather not bring it to the hospital, if that's okay with you. Why don't you come up to the apartment and I can give it to you there? It's really not necessary to have your mom repair it, though."

"It is to me. And if you're okay with it, I'll come up. It will save you the trip back down."

Why the hell had he just offered to do that? Hadn't he just thought how glad he'd be to have her out of sight?

"Okay, great." Still keeping her arm across her dress, she turned sideways and tried to hit the button on her seat belt, struggling with getting her hand that far back.

Roque reached over to hit the release latch for her, his sleeve brushing her bare arm as he did and catching a light floral scent that seemed to cling to her skin. He swallowed. "Wait there."

Getting his cane from the back and climbing out of the car, he came around to her side, the tension in his jaw making itself known in his leg. He leaned a little of his weight on the cane's handle. No wonder he'd stepped on her dress. Maybe this was some elaborate joke perpetrated by karma after his response to his mom's nudging at dinner last night. She'd asked about him meeting someone special. He'd bluntly told her he wasn't interested in meeting anyone—special or not so special. Less than twenty-four hours later, he'd stepped on someone's dress and found his thoughts riveted to all kinds of "what if" scenarios.

Well, he needed to un-rivet them. *Now.*

He forced his steps to quicken, opening her door and pulling the webbing of the seat belt away from her, taking care not to touch her, this time. "Can you get out on your own?"

Deus do céu, he hoped she could.

She swung her legs out of the car and planted them on the ground, but his low-slung car wasn't helping her.

"Here. Give me your hand." He gritted his teeth and forced himself to add the obvious, "The left one."

You're a funny, funny guy, Roque. As if she's going to give you the other one.

She let him pull her up from her seat, her grip on his firm and warm and lingering maybe a second longer than necessary. Then stood in front of him, her head tilted to look at him, the overhead lights shining on cheeks that were slightly pink and far too appealing. "Thanks, I appreciate it."

"The least I can do." And it was. Especially since his thoughts were now having to run some pretty impressive evasive maneuvers, like a footballer trying to stay just out of reach of his opponent. Which in this case happened to be common sense.

She followed him to the elevator. His steps still felt a little off, but he draped his cane over his arm. And he wasn't quite sure why. He wasn't ashamed of that hitch in his stride. Was he?

And when he'd stepped on her dress. Was he being prideful by not using it? And if he had used it, could he have avoided this whole damn mess?

"Did you hurt your foot?"

Her question came out of nowhere, seeming to echo his earlier musings as the elevator doors opened. "What floor are you on?" He stalled for a few seconds, trying to collect his thoughts.

"Four." She licked her lips. "I'm sorry. I shouldn't have asked that."

"No, it's okay." He pushed the button for

her floor, and leaned against the wall to look at her. Her arm was pressed against the neckline of her dress, and he noticed two tiny scars on her hand. Very lickable scars.

Hell, where had that come from?

He forced his attention back to her question. "My injury... It seems I am not only good at tripping over dresses, but my own two feet. It's an old sports' injury."

"Which sport?" Her gaze flicked over his chest, down his abdomen...

He cleared a throat that was suddenly dry. *"Futebol."*

Her eyes were now on his thighs and it was as if she could see right through his clothes. And pretty soon, she was going to see something that was visible despite his clothing.

"Have you had physical therapy?"

The shock of her question hit him like a bucket of ice water, scalding him in a way that heat couldn't touch. If she only knew. Yes, he'd had therapy. And more therapy. All it had done was pile more grief onto an already existing wound. It seemed every female he met thought they could magically fix him and put him back to rights.

His jaw tightened until twin points of pain appeared. "Are you offering me your professional services, Amy?" He made it as clear as he could that she was overstepping her boundaries.

"No. I'm sorry. You're an orthopedist. Of course you have."

"It happened a lifetime ago. And it's permanent. What you see is what you, and everyone else, gets. All the physical therapy in the world won't change it."

Diabos. Why had he gone on the attack? She was trying to help. She wasn't like his ex-therapist or any of those women he'd gone out with who'd shown a morbid interest in his damaged leg.

He moved a step closer, so he could touch her hand. "I'm sorry. That came out badly."

They arrived on the fourth floor before he could explain further. She got out in a hurry and stuck her key into the lock of the nearest door, only to jiggle it. She took it out and tried again. "That's weird. It worked earlier. I'm not sure why it's not this—"

The door opened, and the doctor from the gala appeared.

Amy recoiled a step. "I'm so sorry. I must have the wrong…" She glanced at the key. "Heavens, I do. The key says 402. I've only been up here once."

Lara had a glass of wine in her hand, and when her eyes met his, they widened.

Perfect. She was probably wondering what he was doing coming up to Amy's apartment straight from the party.

As was he.

Should he tell her why? That he'd almost ripped Amy's dress off her at the party and had now come here so she could remove it the rest of the way? That sounded pretty damning actually.

"There were no cabs left." The lie flew off Amy's tongue with incredible speed. Evidently she wasn't any more anxious to give the real reason for his visit than he was. But anyone who'd thought about it long enough would realize, there'd been a whole fleet of taxis parked outside the venue. Even if there were no cabs, it didn't explain why he'd come up in the elevator with her. Or why the strap to her dress had suddenly disappeared. Maybe Lara hadn't noticed how she was dressed.

Amy's chest rose as she took a deep breath. "And actually, my dress strap ripped, and Roque's mother is a professional seamstress, so he offered to have her sew it back together for me."

He blinked. She'd backtracked. Why?

"Oh, that was nice of you," Lara murmured.

"Anyway, sorry for disturbing you. See you in the morning."

The other woman smiled at them and said good night, closing the door and leaving them alone in the corridor.

Roque couldn't contain a grin. "I've never known anyone who can make even the truth sound like a lie."

But when she swung around to look at him, her face was white as a ghost.

She whispered, "You don't care that she might think we've come up here to...?"

He wasn't about to admit that he'd entertained a thought or two himself.

"No. I really don't. I don't worry about what people think of me."

At least he hadn't until a minute ago when he saw the look on her face.

"My mom was like that. It must be pretty freeing."

"Freeing? I don't understand."

"Never mind." Amy moved to the next door down, double-checking the number, and inserted her key into the lock. This time it turned smoothly, opening to a white-tiled corridor and living room just beyond it. She entered, motioning him in behind her.

Roque followed her into the space, glancing around.

"Make yourself at home. I'll just go and change. There's not much in the refrigerator, since I haven't made it to the grocery yet."

"It's okay. I don't need anything."

Her suitcases were in the living room and one of them was open wide, a pair of— *diabos!*—lacy pink briefs hanging over the side of it. His gut immediately tightened and all the thoughts he'd banished came rushing back, followed by a few thousand more.

She hurried over and kicked the offending garment into the case and quickly folded it closed.

What she couldn't close was the part of his brain that had imprinted itself with that image, making him wonder what other forbidden wonders she had hidden in her luggage.

Which was none of his business.

Setting her bags upright, she wheeled one of them toward a room to her left. "I won't be a minute." With that, she shut the door with a thump.

Her panties!

She leaned against the back of the door, shutting her eyes in horror.

Oh, God, they'd been lying there right in front of him! Not minutes after being seen—and recognized—by her neighbor, someone she would have to work with day in and day out. At least for the first month and a half.

But her underwear! Why had she left that case open?

Well, she hadn't expected to have a man in her apartment on her first night.

Or the second or third nights. And now

that she knew who was living next door, probably no other night, either. Any hook-ups would now have to happen "off campus," so to speak.

Roque might not care what people thought, but she did. Far too much. And she certainly didn't want him to hear secondhand that she was entertaining men in one of the hospital's apartments.

Entertaining men? What was this? The 1920s?

Opening her eyes, she went over to the bed and hefted her suitcase onto it, one-handed. This was ridiculous. He couldn't see her now. She let go of her dress, and sure enough, the top of her bodice slid past her waist. Quickly finding a pair of yoga pants and a loose-fitting T-shirt, she opened the side zipper on her dress and let it slither the rest of the way down.

There, are you happy now?

She glared at the garment at her feet, stepping out of it and tossing it onto the bed with a little more force than was necessary.

She then dug through her bag, aware of a little time clock ticking in her head as she tried to find her bra. She blinked. She'd worn one on the flight over, so it had to be here somewhere. Or another one. That maybe she'd packed in the other suitcase that was still in the living room. Or not?

Ack. She'd left the bra she'd traveled in in the bathroom when she'd changed for the party, since she hadn't needed it for the dress. She was not leaving this room to go grab it and waltz her way back to the bedroom with it dangling from her fingertips. That would be almost worse than him seeing her underwear. Although maybe he hadn't noticed.

Oh, he'd noticed, all right. His eyes had been right on them.

So what to do? She'd always been small up top, wishing as a teenager that she had more oomph in that department. But right now, she was glad she didn't. She pulled the T-shirt over her head. It was black and loose. Peering into the bedroom mirror, she decided you couldn't really tell as long as you weren't staring at her chest.

So hauling her yoga pants up over her hips and sliding her feet into a pair of flip-flops, she took the decorative comb out of her hair, tired of it digging into her scalp.

"I don't worry about what people think of me." Wasn't that what he'd said?

Well, maybe she could practice a little of what he—and her mom—preached. She shook her hair out, trying not to care that it was curling in all kinds of crazy directions. She then folded her dress in as small a ball as possible and shoved it into one of the plastic grocery bags she'd included in case she had any wet clothes to pack on the return flight.

There. She was ready.

Sucking down a quick breath, she opened the door and sauntered into the living room as if she hadn't a care in the world. As soon as she saw him, she wished she hadn't agreed to let him take the dress. He was lounging on her sofa, both arms stretched out over the top of it, looking as fresh in his dark suit as the moment she'd laid eyes on him. And she was…

Not caring what people thought, that's what she was.

His glance trailed over her hair, before

arriving at the plastic bag in her hand. "Is that it?"

"Yes." She handed it to him. "Thanks again."

"For ripping your dress?"

Maybe. Could it be that this little mishap had provided a way to break the ice? To give her that little flaw in his perfection that she'd been searching for?

"You make a pretty intimidating figure—did you know that?"

His head cocked. "No. I didn't."

"I think even Peter and Lara felt it." Although he wasn't intimidating in a bad sort of way, like whoever Flávia had been referring to.

"Then I'll have to work on that."

He uncurled himself from the sofa and stood over her, and there it was again. That shiver of awareness. And whether it was because of the T-shirt fabric brushing over her bare skin or her reaction to him, her nipples tightened as a swirl of sensation spiraled down her belly to points below. She had to fight the urge to hook her arm back over her chest like she'd done while holding up her dress.

"You don't have to work on anything. I'm sure it's just part of being in a different country." Why on earth had she said anything to him? "Pretty much everything is intimidating to me right now."

"Don't be intimidated, Amy. You'll find Brazilians are quite *amigáveis.*"

"I know they're friendly. I didn't really mean that."

"What did you mean, then?"

"I'm not sure. I just feel a little bit out of place. Everyone I've met has been either a doctor or an expert in their field."

"You are an expert in your field, or you wouldn't be here."

She hadn't thought of it like that. She'd heard the vetting process was tough and was actually surprised that she'd gotten in, even if it had been because someone else had dropped out. "Well, thank you. But not really."

"Don't sell yourself short. The team decided you were right for this position."

Something caught her attention. "The team. But not you?"

"The heads of the departments are given a list of applicants that are *préselecionados*... I think you say it as 'short-listed,' yes? And then the selections are made. You were on that list."

He was evading the question about whether or not he had wanted her. Or was he?

"But I only got on afterward, when there was a cancellation."

"There was no cancellation. The powers that be were merely trying to find where best to place you. The physical therapy department couldn't spare anyone to oversee your month-and-a-half shadow period. So you are now with me. I almost said no. Until I read one of your case files. It made me change my mind."

He almost refused to work with her? And if he had, she'd still be sitting in the States.

She did not want him to see how much that stung.

He changed his mind, Amy. That counts for something.

"Which case file?"

"The spina bifida patient who went on to practice martial arts."

Bobby Sellers. She almost hadn't included him, because he hadn't been the stellar success story she felt the hospital was looking for. But he'd touched her life. And when he told her he'd always wanted to break a board in tae kwon do, something her mom had insisted on her participating in, it had struck a chord. And she'd helped him work toward that, even going as far as attending the event where Bobby had indeed broken his board. It had brought her to tears.

"But why that case?"

"It showed that you are able to think outside the box—that you don't keep pushing where it will do no good. You tweaked the prescribing doctor's treatment plan slightly to include your patient's own personal life goals. That is exactly what I want to see at Paulista. Things don't always follow a prescribed path. As the saying goes, medicine is sometimes more art than science."

"I believe that as well. We have to look at patients as a whole, not as a conglomeration of symptoms. We have to help them adapt and change when the body won't cooperate."

He smiled and stood, leaning on his cane a little more than he had been. "And *that* is why I said yes. I should go. *I* might not care about what people think, but I have a feeling you do. And since Dr. Smith knows I'm here in your apartment..."

Yes, it was time for Roque to go. But not because of Lara Smith. Or the fact that the pink scrap of lace peeking out of her suitcase was going to haunt him for days to come. He was pretty sure she wasn't wearing a bra under that T-shirt. But none of that was what drove him to say goodbye. It was because of the vulnerability he'd seen in her when they were talking about how she'd gotten into the program.

He'd sensed a bit of imposter syndrome, and he probably had fueled that even more with his honesty. But he hadn't wanted to work with someone like the physical therapist he'd been assigned after his surgery. He didn't want a fix-it mentality. He wanted someone with the ability to set realistic expectations for his or her patients. In the end, Roque would not have agreed, if the candidate absolutely didn't meet that qualification. His patients were too important to him.

But to have stepped on her dress.

Hell. He definitely did not have the co-ordination he'd had back in his days with Chutegol, his football club. But then again, his injury had resulted in muscle and nerve damage, and although you wouldn't know it from the single long scar on his outer thigh, the damage to the underlying structures had ended his football career. Fortunately, he'd earned enough from his five years of playing to put himself through medical school.

"Well, thank you for coming."

Amy's voice cut through the fog of his thoughts, and he swung his gaze to her, avoiding looking at her chest.

"I will let you know when it is done." He held up the bag containing the real reason he was here. His mother would be happy to repair it for her. But not without a question or two, or a mention of their earlier conversation, which made him wonder if he'd been right to offer her services. After having women throw themselves at him during his football days, and the messy breakup of his engagement, and then the pass his physical therapist had made during treatment, he was leery of believing someone could be interested in *him*...as someone who came from simple roots, who'd worked hard for everything he had. So his relationships were short and sweet, and very, very superficial. No one who would try to "fix" whatever they thought was wrong with him.

So yes, his mother would ask some pointed questions.

But Roque took care of the mistakes that he could. And the ones he couldn't? Well, he walked away from them.

Amy wrapped her arms around her midsection. "The dress was my fault, so don't worry about it. Like I said, it's too long. I shouldn't have worn it."

The image of her with her forearm clamped across her chest to keep her bodice from falling down swam in front of his face. Were all her undergarments pink? And lacy?

Damn. Talk about mistakes. Maybe this was a bigger one than he realized.

"The dress was—*is*—quite lovely." His phone buzzed on his hip. Glancing at the readout, he frowned. Enzo Dos Santos? He hadn't heard from the owner of the football club in ages, other than a quick note saying he'd had a cancerous lesion removed from his jaw. Had things gone south? He let the call go to voice mail, making a note to call his friend back once he got back to the car. "I'll let you know when my mom has had a chance to look at it."

What he wouldn't tell her was the hoops he was sure to have to jump through before his mom actually got down to work.

"Well, thank you again."

"You're welcome. I'll see you in the morning." Roque had been dreading this three-month rotation, but there was now a weird sense of anticipation he hadn't felt in a while. One he didn't like and halfway suspected was due to the woman whose dress he'd stepped on. She was here for three months. Why risk letting things get messy, when they could stay in a neat and tidy box. And where he'd have no more mistakes to correct. So he said his goodbyes and walked out of her apartment, glancing at Lara's door and wondering if she was staring out her peephole with a stop watch. Ridiculous. Roque did not care what people thought.

Except for the owner of his former football team. When he got to his car, he tossed Amy's dress into the passenger seat and slid into the vehicle, taking out his phone and scrolling through his missed messages. Then putting all thoughts of his rotation charge out of his head, he dialed Enzo's number and waited for the man to pick up his phone.

CHAPTER THREE

HE'D GIVEN HER a choice. Take the morning off or scrub in on an emergency Achilles' tendon surgery.

It had been an easy choice. Scrub for surgery.

The surgical mask felt strange and confining, but it was also a different experience. She could now see why people said the eyes were the window to the soul.

Roque glanced at her, brows raised. "Are you sure you wish to be here?"

"Absolutely." She wondered why Lara and Peter were not in the room as well. Maybe because they both saw surgical procedures day in and day out, and a complete rupture of the tendon was probably no big deal for them. But it was to her. It would give her a glimpse into what went on before a patient arrived on her physical therapy table.

"Let me know if you have any questions, since I'll be speaking in Portuguese once we start. I'm going to do a percutaneous repair rather than opening his leg, to reduce the chance of infection."

"And if you need to graft part of the tendon?"

He looked surprised. "Good question. This case is fairly straightforward. If the ends of the tendon were say…shredded, I would then open the leg and fold down a portion of the *gastrocnêmio*… In English—?"

"Gastrocnemius?"

"Yes, that is it."

The corners of his eyes crinkled in a smile that made her swallow. Without being able to see his mouth or the rest of his face, and with his emotions being translated by his eyes, it forced her to watch carefully. That had to be why her own senses were taking in every millimeter of movement and multiplying how it affected her.

"We would use a portion of that tissue to

reinforce the repair. To make it less likely to rupture a second time."

"But you don't need to this time?"

"No. This patient is still in school and young and healthy. He should be able to return to football, once he lets the injury heal completely." He glanced around the surgical room where the other personnel appeared to be waiting on a signal from him. "Let's get started. You can ask more questions as we go."

She answered with a quick nod.

His words hadn't been a dismissal. So why had it felt that way? Maybe because she knew he'd almost said no to her being in the program. And because she'd been way too caught up in their exchange of words and hadn't been quite ready to end it.

A natural reaction, Amy.

Of course she'd be interested in learning as much as she could. And she wanted to show Roque that she absolutely should be here, despite any reservations he might have had in the beginning.

The orthopedist walked over to the patient who was already prepped for surgery and under general anesthesia. He motioned for her to join him by the table, while a nurse with a tray of surgical instruments stood on his other side. Amy watched as he made two tiny incisions on either side of the leg, using forceps to enlarge the holes slightly. He gave a running commentary in Portuguese, which she surprisingly understood, only missing a word or two here and there. "I'm going to place sutures under the skin in a figure-eight motion, catching the upper part of the tendon and using the suture material to draw it down to meet the other half."

He then ran the needle through the first of the incisions and out the second hole. When he ducked back in, he allowed the point of the needle to tell him where to make the next small cut, repeating the process down the leg until he reached the other end of the tendon. His long fingers were sure and precise, almost dancing over the surface of his patient's skin.

Not a good analogy, because her brain immediately opened up a side-by-side screen, putting her where Roque's patient was, with those fingers sliding up the back of one of her calves in a way that had nothing to do with surgery. She blinked away the image, trying to force her eyes to focus on what was happening in front of her.

"Almost done."

Amy glanced up at the clock, shocked to see that only about ten minutes had gone by. And the procedure was a lot more straightforward than she'd expected it to be. Somehow he found the tendon under the skin without any kind of imaging equipment, seeming to go by feel. But there'd been no hesitation. How many of these had he done over the course of his career? Enough to make it seem like a piece of cake.

Roque tugged on the two ends of suture line and she could almost see the ends of the tendon pulling together beneath the patient's skin, just like the ripped seams of her dress's strap would be pulled back together as his mom stitched it. An odd comparison, but it really was what had happened. Only this man's leg was alive, and a ripped tendon couldn't just be cast aside like a piece of clothing.

"These sutures are absorbable, whereas

the ones I'll put on the outside will need to be removed." He tied off the inner stitches, and was handed another threaded needle, which he used to close each of the tiny holes he'd made in the skin. He glanced at her. "And that's it. Not very exciting."

Yes, it was. Too exciting actually. But not in the way he meant. Roque's eyes were brown, but without his dark clothing on, they had almost an amber hue that she hadn't caught last night. Or maybe because she'd been too busy taking in the man as a whole rather than being fixated on one small part of him.

No, not fixated. But when she scrambled around for another word, she suddenly couldn't find one.

That was a problem for later, because she couldn't exactly think straight right now.

"Thanks for letting me watch the procedure. I've done the physio for several Achilles' reattachment patients. It's a long slow process in the States."

He nodded, pulling his mask down and thanking his team, before responding. The curve of his mouth set off a line in his left cheek that had probably been a dimple when he was a child.

He wasn't a child anymore, though. He was all man.

"The process is long here as well. Andreu, our patient, won't be able to play for six months and will be in a boot for several weeks."

She sighed. "Six months can seem like forever to someone so young."

"Yes. It can seem like a lifetime. But at least *his* outcome should be a good one."

The cryptic words made her heart ache, because she knew who he was referring to.

As he moved toward the back of the room, his steps seemed a little slower, the hitch she'd noticed earlier was more pronounced. He'd left his cane outside, probably to avoid contaminating the room. It was on the tip of her tongue to offer to go ahead of him and retrieve it for him, but no one else in the room had volunteered. Maybe it was a touchy subject. And as a physical therapist, she knew that the more people could do for themselves, the better.

A thought struck her. "Was this your first surgery of the day?"

"No, my third."

"What?" She pulled off her own mask and gloves, discarding them in the trash can next to the door and glancing at the clock on the wall. "It's barely eight-thirty."

"There was an accident involving a *moto-taxi* in the early hours. The driver and his passenger both had multiple injuries."

His specialty was sports medicine, but obviously he handled regular ortho surgeries as well. "Are they okay?"

"The passenger will make it, but the driver…" He shook his head.

"Oh, no. My mom said that motorcyclists here have a dangerous life, but I'm sure that's true everywhere."

"It is very true here." He pushed through the door and took his cane, leaning on it for a minute. "Do you mind if we grab a coffee? Peter and Lara aren't due in until noon, and I have a long day ahead of me."

"You don't have to babysit me, if you need to go grab a catnap."

"Cat…nap?"

Oh! Of course he wouldn't know that phrase. "A light sleep? *Soneca?*"

"But why a cat?"

"I don't know. The cat we had when I was growing up slept a lot, and her sleep wasn't exactly light."

He smiled, and started walking, using his cane on every fourth step or so. "It's the same with mine."

He had a cat?

She blinked. Somehow she didn't picture him as a cat person, although she wasn't sure why. But the image of him baby-talking to a sulky feline made her giggle. She quickly swallowed it when he gave her a sideways look.

"Something is funny?"

"No. I was just surprised you have a cat."

"Yes. Me too. I… Let's say I inherited her from someone."

"Your parents?" Her childhood cat had died not long after her mom passed away. The second loss had hit her hard, since her mom had loved Tabby fiercely.

"No. Not my parents."

The gritted words sounded pained, although he hadn't increased his reliance on his cane. Oh. A girlfriend. Or a wife.

"I'm sorry. I shouldn't have asked."

"It's okay. My fiancée considered Rachel her cat. But when we broke up...well, let's just say there were allergies involved. So the cat stayed with me."

Allergies were involved in the breakup? No, that didn't make sense. Her eyes widened. The girlfriend had either cheated or found someone else soon after they broke off their relationship. Someone who was allergic to cats.

That's a whole lot of speculating, Amy.

But the curt way he spoke about it said the split hadn't been exactly amicable. "Well, I'm glad you didn't take the kitty to a shelter."

"There are very few shelters here. But I still wouldn't have. Rachel was originally a street cat, but has adapted very well to life inside my apartment."

She could imagine why. A shot of warmth pulsed through her.

And Roque had evidently adapted very well to life with a cat. Somehow the idea of Roque squatting down to pick up some terrified, emaciated cat and comforting her made a wave of emotion well up inside of her. She'd always been a sucker for a man who was kind to animals. And to name his cat Rachel?

That was probably the doing of the fiancée as well. "How did she get her name?"

"There was a certain American program that my fiancée liked. It revolved around a café."

She'd binge-watched it with her mom. "That's a classic. Have you seen it?"

"I couldn't much avoid it." There went that tension in his jaw again. And there went her stomach.

Thankfully they arrived at the hospital's coffee shop, a trendy looking café that would rival the one in the TV show. "That looks great."

"What do you want?"

"I can get it."

"It's on the hospital."

It was? She didn't remember coffee breaks being covered. "A skinny vanilla latte, please."

She could see the wheels in his head turning as he puzzled through the words, so she tried again. "A latte with nonfat milk?"

"Ah...skinny. Nonfat milk, I see."

"What is it in Brazil?"

"*Leite desnatada*...literally de-creamed milk."

She laughed. "That makes sense."

Roque went to the counter and placed their orders, while she found a seat in the far corner. With cozy upholstered armchairs flanking a wood-topped table, the place had the feeling of a living room, where friends met to talk.

Not that she and Roque were friends, or ever would be anything more than acquaintances. He was in charge of...yes, babysitting her—until she, Lara and Peter were done with this three months. And with how slow this second day was going it might seem like forever by the end of her stay.

Dropping into her seat with a sigh, she studied her surroundings. The coffee shop overlooked the lower level of the hospital, where people were busy coming and going, including a group of medical students in white lab coats. Someone was in front of them, explaining the accoutrements of the hospital. There was another couple seated at a neighboring table. By the tiny touches and long, sultry looks, they were a pair. The sight made her heart cramp.

Amy's last relationship had left her wary of investing anything of value—like her heart. And she certainly wasn't going to start something she couldn't finish while she was in São Paulo.

Which is why she'd thought about just having a quick, casual bout of sex.

Bout? She made it sound like an illness, not something sexy and fun.

Roque came back to the table with an espresso cup, a shot glass with some kind of clear liquid and her taller latte. *"Café com leite desnatada e baunilha."* There were also two wrapped pieces of biscotti on the plate.

Wow, he could even make coffee sound sensual. She touched a finger to the shot glass. "What is this?"

"Seltzer water. It clears the palate and helps the flavor of the coffee come through."

Okay, she'd definitely heard of seltzer

water, but had never actually seen anyone use it for that.

He passed her drink over, along with the wrapped biscotti, and sat in one of the other seats, leaning his cane against the wall behind him.

"Sometimes you use that and sometimes you don't," she said, mentally kicking herself for bringing it up again.

"My leg gets tired and cramps up. After the break in my femur was repaired, the leg developed an infection, so I lost some of the muscle. It doesn't bother me all that much, but it's either use the cane or fall on my face from time to time."

"Sorry, I don't know why I keep asking about it. It's none of my business."

"You're curious. It's natural." One side of his mouth tilted at a crazy angle. "Believe me. I will not have a problem with telling you if you step over a line."

Like the question about his fiancée that kept buzzing around her head like a pesky mosquito? What kind of woman would Roque be attracted to? Oh, Lord, she was not about to ask about her. She didn't want to know anything about their relationship, or why it had failed. She was pretty sure he would pull her up short if she even mentioned it.

She took a sip of her coffee and focused on the flavor instead. It was mellow with low rich tones that blended perfectly with the milk and vanilla. "Oh, this is good."

Maybe it was the presentation—the glass showing the color to perfection...and that thick layer of foam on the top. Whatever it was, it tasted so much better than what she could buy in coffee shops back home. Or maybe it was just the fact that she was actually drinking coffee in Brazil. Brazil! It had been one of her dreams for a very long time.

"You have something..." One of his long fingers touched the left side of his upper lip. *"Espuma."*

Sponge? Oh! Foam—from the milk. She touched her tongue to the area and swept it back and forth a couple of times. "Gone?"

His gaze slowly tracked back up, and he took a visible swallow. Their eyes met. Held. They stayed that way for a long, long minute before he said, "Yes. It is gone." His voice

had an odd timbre to it, sounding almost…
wistful.

No. Not wistful. He didn't seem like the
type of man to engage in…well, fluff.

He did have a cat, though, which she
hadn't expected, either.

Roque unwrapped his biscotti and took a
bite, watching her as she took another sip.
This time she was a little more careful with
the frothy top layer. "Do you have more surgeries today?"

"Later. I need to check in on my *moto* patient and the Achilles patient first. You're
welcome to tag along if you'd like." He
drank the rest of the contents of his demi-
tasse cup.

One of his patients today had died, from
what he'd implied. He had to be emotion-
ally exhausted. Not wanting to add anything
onto him, she shook her head. "I think I'll
do a little exploring of the hospital, if that's
okay. I can meet you at noon, when Lara and
Peter arrive. Where do you want to meet?"

"How about right here." He glanced at his
watch. "I'll see my patients, and then I might
have that kitty-nap you talked about."

She smiled. And for the first time it felt real and unselfconscious. He was trying to use new words and not worrying about whether they were right or wrong, so maybe she should get off her high horse and be a little more adventurous. She blinked. In the language department, of course.

"I think you mean *cat*nap."

"Kitty-nap does not mean the same thing?"

"No, it doesn't mean anything, really. And I do think you should take some time to rest. You look…" Tired. That's what she'd been going to say. Not gorgeous. Not dreamy. Or any of the other crazy adjectives that were now crawling around the dark spaces of her skull.

"I look…?"

He tilted his head and regarded her as if maybe reading her mind. *Ack!* Time to think of something really unflattering.

"Kind of wrung-out."

His head stayed tilted, but now a frown appeared between his brows. He didn't understand what she meant.

"It means very tired. Exhausted."

"Ah, yes. I do feel a little tired." His

glance dropped back to her lips before he suddenly climbed to his feet. "You will be okay on your own?"

Maybe she should have felt insulted that he would ask her that. But she was in a different culture and she knew it. And actually, she appreciated his concern.

And the fact that he'd just been looking at her mouth again? She wasn't going to check for foam. Not this time. Because it would just dig her in deeper. She needed to be by herself for a little while so she could regain her composure, which was being tested to the limit right now.

"I'll be fine, thank you. I have an uncle in São Paulo. I'd like to see if I can find him. I'm hoping he's still at the old address I have for him."

"Would you like help tracking him down?"

She would actually. She had no idea how to go about it, other than go to his last known address. But to just show up at the door? "Maybe. When you have time. I'm more worried about the language barrier than anything."

"I do not think it will be much of a barrier. But I will be happy to go with you, if you'd like."

She hadn't expected that. But the relief that went through her was so great that it was a struggle not to let it show. "Yes. I would like that. Thank you so much!"

He gathered their cups and saucers and started to turn toward the counter when he took a wrong step and very nearly tumbled. Her latte glass fell and shattered on the tile floor below.

"Maldito!"

Compassion poured through her, pushing aside her relief and everything else. "It's okay, hand me the other things and I'll get it." She took them out of his hands and went down on her haunches.

He made no move to kneel down to help pick up the big shards of glass, and she realized he either couldn't or he was worried that he might not be able to get up without help. And for someone like Roque, that thought was probably unbearable. He'd said he used his cane when his leg got tired. Well, if he was exhausted, that affected muscle was probably giving him fits.

The barista came over with a broom and dustpan. She murmured to let her get it and in short order had everything swept and tidy once again, taking the rest of their plates and cups and carrying everything over to the bar.

"I'm sorry."

"You don't have to be, Roque. I could have just as easily dropped them myself."

"But you didn't."

She touched his hand. "We've all been there."

"Have you?" This time there was a touch of anger in his voice. He thought she was patronizing him. But she wasn't. Yes, he had a permanent disability, but that didn't make him any less valuable than the next person. Hadn't she almost tripped over her dress at the welcoming party? More than once?

"Yes. I've dropped things for no good reason. Fallen while jogging. Slipped in the shower. All kinds of things. You're human." She forced a smile, maybe to keep the moisture that had gathered at the back of her eyeballs from moving toward the front. "Even if you don't want to believe it."

In a move that shocked her, his hand turned, capturing hers in his warm grip for several long seconds. Her heart picked up its pace until it was almost pounding in her ears.

"Of being human, I have no doubts. But thank you."

"You're very welcome. Now go get some rest. I'll see you at noon."

He let go and gave a quick nod, reaching for his cane. "I will. If you have any questions, just stop and ask someone. Our staff is always happy to help."

She'd noticed that from the time she'd arrived. But not just the hospital. Brazilians in general were a very friendly people. "I will, thank you."

With that, Roque turned and started to make his way across the coffee shop. Only this time, instead of every four or five steps, his cane hit the floor each time he bore weight on his left leg. It really was hurting him.

Damn, maybe she really should suggest he get some PT done. Or at least a deep tissue massage to give that damaged muscle a way to recuperate some energy.

What was the worst he could say?

That she'd crossed over that invisible line.

Even if he knew she could offer him some relief?

She had a feeling it wasn't just about the pain, or whatever else he was experiencing. It was about his pride. Something that Amy was all too aware of. She could remember people wanting to help her after her mom passed away and waving them off like it was no big deal. Like people lost their moms every single day. Even as she felt like she was dying inside.

So maybe she would just have to somehow make him think it was his idea.

Really? She didn't think the man was going to come over to her and say, *Hey, could you bring those magic hands over here?*

Ha! No, he wouldn't say it in those words. At all. Because it sounded like too much of a come-on.

Besides, he'd already tried the physical therapy route, he'd said.

Yes, maybe he had. But how long ago was that? There were always new ways of doing things. Probably ways he hadn't tried, depending on how long ago the injury had occurred.

Well, that was something she could think about later. When she had a little space to breathe. Being around him was a lot more disconcerting than it should be, and Amy had no idea why.

But maybe she'd better sit down and try to figure out what it was about him that was putting her off balance, before she spent too many sleepless nights.

Because the sooner she understood why he was affecting her the way he did, the better it would be for her. And for him.

CHAPTER FOUR

ROQUE PUNCHED HIS pillow one more time, then dropped back onto it, propping his hands behind his head. He still couldn't figure out why he'd offered to go to Amy's uncle's house with her.

He'd analyzed every possible "why" over the last two days and had marked them off one by one: first explanation, she didn't know the language. Oh, yes, she did. Enough to understand almost everything that was said to her. Second possibility, he worried about her going out alone in some areas of the city. This was true to some extent, except they had the summer lecture program every year, and he had never felt the need to babysit anyone that came through the program. Third, those damned pink briefs that had been hanging out of the suitcase at her apartment. He leaped quickly over that possibility and headed straight for reason number four: there was an uncertainty about her that pulled at his gut. And this was the heart of the matter and something that had kept him up until well after midnight tonight, despite his killer of a day.

Maybe she would decide not to go and let him off the hook. Or maybe she would go without him.

He shut his eyes. Despite the awkward awareness that refused to die, and as much as he might regret offering—and even after all his tossing and turning, he wasn't sure he did—he did want to help her. At least in this one thing.

There. That was the solution. It was one outing. One good deed out of several years' worth of participating in this program. And anyway, she was nothing like the physical therapist that had made a pass at him in those early years of therapy. As long as she didn't offer to treat him, he was fine.

With that settled, Roque finally rested fully against his pillow, realizing for the first time how tense he'd been. He mentally visited each muscle group, limb by limb, and consciously forced them to relax.

He sucked in a deep breath and blew it out, allowing the darkness of the room to seep into him, doing his best to will his subconscious to do the same. Maybe then he could finally get a few hours of sleep, before the new day found him.

Three days down, eighty-seven days to go.

Oh, Lord. That was a lot of days. Amy rotated her neck and tried to work the odd kink out of it. At least things hadn't been too bad yesterday after Roque had met up with the rest of their little group.

She came in through the double doors at the front of the hospital and showed her ID to the guard stationed by the gate.

At his nod, she passed through it, heading toward the elevators and seeing several people were already there.

Oh! Krysta was waving her over. And there was Flávia. She reached them. "I think I'm having a case of déjà vu. Only I wasn't this tired at the welcome party."

"We were just talking about how fast-paced everything is here in São Paulo."

"Did you already do your seminars?" Krysta and Flávia were scheduled to speak on their respective areas. "I haven't even looked at the lineup yet."

"No." Both women answered at once and they laughed. Krysta glanced at the elevator panel that sat out front. "Which floor are you headed to?"

"Fourth. I'm meeting Roque Cardoza."

"Is he the one you were sitting by at the party?"

"Yep. He's in charge of me for the next couple of weeks. I have to do anything he says, evidently."

Both women's heads swiveled toward her, and she realized they'd taken that the wrong way. "I mean related to the job."

"Com certeza. Só o trabalho." Flávia's voice had a touch of mirth in it. "It's not like he's hard to look at. If that's your thing."

A flame seemed to lick up Amy's face and ignite her cheeks. "You guys… I don't think of him like that at all. Besides, he's really *not* all that good-looking."

Liar.

Ping!

"Looks like that's your elevator," Flávia said. "And here's mine. See you both soon."

Seconds later Amy slid into the elevator, just as Roque showed up behind her, his cane draped over his arm today. When she glanced up, she caught a half smile on his lips. Oh, no. Surely he hadn't heard what they'd been talking about. Her face sizzled in mortification. "How are you?"

"I guess it depends on what part of me you're talking about?"

He had! He'd overheard them. "You... Were you standing behind us?"

"Only long enough to hear how not attractive you find me."

If she thought her face had been hot before, it was now an inferno. One she wished would consume her and turn her into a pile of ash.

But there was no way she would be that lucky. "Sorry. I didn't know what else to say." And thank heavens she hadn't sat there and gushed over him or worse.

"I'm glad, actually, that you don't think

of me like that, because it could complicate things while you're here. It's much better to stick to the business at hand."

Something she was having a difficult time doing, although she wasn't sure why.

"Of course. I wouldn't want it any other way."

"So, the team is already upstairs waiting on us."

The rest of the ride was spent talking about cases and how her physical therapy would be used over the next several weeks. A little thrill of excitement went through her that had nothing to do with Roque, this time. At least, she hoped it didn't.

"I actually have an old friend who will be at the hospital shortly," he said. "He is going to have his mandible rebuilt after cancer surgery. He'll be looking to do physical therapy afterward, and I'd like you to handle the case."

"Me?" The elevator doors opened.

"Yes. He's had a hard go of it, and our physical therapy staff is stretched thin after a couple of therapists transferred to another hospital. His wife is English, and he has an excellent grasp of the language."

He'd mentioned kind of inheriting her because of how busy things were in the PT department.

"I'll help however I can, of course." She thought for a second. "How much of his jaw was removed?"

"Enough to make it a challenge to reconstruct it. But Krysta Simpson is more than up to the challenge, from what I understand. Our own Dr. Francisco Carvalho will be working with her on this—you'll probably meet him at some point in time. There was a bit of a glitch, but hopefully that's been ironed out."

"Glitch?"

"One of our senior oncologists wanted to take over the case, but that was pretty quickly squashed by all involved, as well as by the hospital administrator. Paulista isn't without its own share of…how do you put it? Drama?"

Flávia's comment about a snake that walked on two legs came back to her. But she wasn't sure of the man's name, so it probably wouldn't be good to ask. "Anything I should steer clear of?"

"I wouldn't think so…but if for some reason a doctor you don't know stops by once the patient starts doing physical therapy, I would appreciate a quick text or call. It's not that he'll do anything wrong, I just don't want Enzo put through anything more than he's already endured."

"Of course, I completely understand."

He nodded off toward the waiting area. "There they are, shall we?"

Today, Roque's steps were firm and sure, and her thoughts of trying to talk him into a massage or a little additional PT flew out the window. Maybe it really was only when he was tired. But watching him carefully, she thought she saw a hint of a limp, still, but it was small enough that she could have been mistaken.

He glanced back. "Coming?"

Lordy. She'd been standing staring at him as he walked. She hurried to catch up, then greeted Peter and Lara, and set out to put her mind completely on work.

* * *

She didn't think he was all that good-looking?

It shouldn't have stung, but after being up half the night thinking about her, Roque's head kept replaying the words she'd said to her friends. And hell if it didn't bother him. Maybe because he thought the woman was gorgeous with a capital G. And her smile…

Damn.

Maybe he just didn't "do it for her," or worse, maybe it was his leg. His ex had certainly changed her tune as soon as she found out he'd never play *futebol* again. She hadn't been able to get out of that hospital room quickly enough, even though she'd said it was because she needed to go and get some clean clothes, so she could stay in the room with him. Only she hadn't stayed. She'd come back for a few more visits. But once he got home, she said she wanted to give him space to recover.

She evidently needed her space as well… for something else entirely. Because not long afterward she'd broken it off, saying she was sorry but she'd fallen in love with someone

else—that it had happened before he was injured. She wouldn't tell him who it was.

But then the tabloids had picked up the story and shouted the news to the world: Halee Fonseca, queen of Brazil's telenovelas, had dumped former Chutegol player Roque Cardoza. She was in love with another player. And the "who" would have been laughable if it hadn't been Roque's best friend on the team.

It had been a crushing blow. But who could blame her? She was famous and must have wanted an equally famous spouse. The pair were happily married now with two children. And Carlos had moved up to Roque's spot on the team and was still successfully playing ball.

He shook his head clear of those thoughts. He hadn't thought about Halee in years and wasn't sure what had brought her back to mind. Maybe Amy's comment. One thing he knew, even if his ex came back and wanted to get back together, he'd turn her down. He was well and truly over her.

And if Amy came calling? Would he turn her down as well?

She wouldn't. He'd heard her himself. She didn't think he was all that attractive.

But if she did?

Caramba! She doesn't. Just leave it there, Cardoza!

"Roque?"

Amy had asked a question. One that he'd totally missed. "I'm sorry. Say it again?"

"I asked if your Achilles' tendon patient will come to Paulista for his physical therapy. I'd like to at least watch and see how things differ between here and the States."

"I think you'll find it doesn't differ all that much, which is part of the reason for the yearly lecture series. We study rehabilitation methods from all over the world, as I'm sure you have as well. We adapt the methods to work in our particular situation, but you'll find we're kind of an *amálgama* of all of the world's top hospitals."

And now he sounded defensive...or worse, arrogant, which wasn't what he meant at all. It had to have come from missing sleep last night. All he knew were that his muscles were tightening up all over again. Not a good thing for his damaged leg.

Peter hadn't said much of anything, and Lara's head was tilted as if puzzling through something, maybe sensing a little tension.

A little? Roque had been on edge ever since he stepped on that dress. Which reminded him. His mom had called this morning, saying the repairs on Amy's dress were done. She'd been determined to bring it to the hospital, even though he'd asked her just to drop it by the house. He was too hard to catch there, she'd said. Besides, she wanted to meet this woman whose dress he had.

Why was she so interested? And exactly why was he so uptight about that happening?

Was he afraid she would say something that would embarrass him? Well, his mom *had* dragged out his naked baby pictures and put them up on the big-screen television he'd bought her a year ago, thinking it was hilarious. Not so hilarious was the fact that she still wanted him married. With children. She hadn't exactly hounded him about it, but she brought it up enough to make him roll his eyes. And she'd hated Halee, so he guessed everything had worked out the way it was supposed to.

"I'm sure, which is part of the reason I wanted to come here so badly. It's one thing to read about surgical techniques. It's another thing to see them in person. Just like the beaches here in Brazil." Amy sighed. "I should have planned in some vacation time. But I didn't. So I'll have to squeeze a beach visit in during my working stay somehow."

Peter smiled. "My wife would slay me if I hadn't included her in some vacation time. Which beach are you thinking about?"

"Guarujá actually. It's only fifty miles away from the city and it sounds really beautiful."

"No." The word was out before Roque could stop himself. Everyone stared at him.

"Did I pronounce it wrong?" she asked.

Caramba. No, she hadn't pronounced it wrong. It sounded warm and husky coming out in those low tones of hers. That wasn't the problem. The problem was him…and that particular place.

"Guarujá is beautiful, but it has a reputation, especially this time of year." He suddenly knew what he was going to do. He was going to take his one good deed and make it two. Maybe then he wouldn't feel so awkward about intruding on her reunion with her uncle. He just needed to figure out how to suggest it.

Now she was frowning. "Reputation? It's a nice area, from what I read."

"It is, but…" He thought for a second. "There are quite a few wealthy individuals who live there, and that creates problems, just like it does everywhere. Guarujá can draw those who want to take from them."

Her face cleared. "Point taken. So where would you suggest?"

He glanced at Lara and Peter, deciding he didn't want either of them here for what he was about to suggest. "Would you two mind going on ahead? I left a list of patients I'd like you to look over at the nurses' desk."

Maybe he was wrong, but they both looked a bit relieved to be sent off. He hoped no one was getting the wrong idea about their relationship. Hell, *he* didn't want to get the wrong idea, so he needed to go about this carefully.

"If we can find out if your address is correct for your uncle, maybe we can combine that visit with a trip to Guarujá. How does that sound?"

Innocent enough. Even to his own ears. All he had to do was keep it that way.

"Are you sure? I hate to take any more of your time. You already had to make a trip to my apartment."

Yes, and the glimpse of those damned lacy undergarments still hadn't faded from his memory. Maybe he just needed to replace that memory with others that were less…volatile.

"I don't mind, unless you'd rather go with Lara and Peter."

She tilted her head as if thinking for a second or two. "Actually, your idea is a good one, and neither Lara nor Peter can help with translating for me. I really do appreciate your offering to help with that. Thank you."

"It's not a problem. We'll coordinate times and try to do it on my next scheduled day off."

It had been ages since he'd heard the crash of ocean waves or let the salty breeze flick along his limbs—things he'd learned to love as a child growing up in Rio's Barra da

Tijuca. He'd missed making weekly treks to the beach.

That had to be why he was suddenly looking forward to the thought of spending the day with her. Maybe a little too much. But it was too late to retract the offer now. And he found he didn't want to. Besides, it wasn't like anything would happen. She wasn't even attracted to him from what he'd overheard her saying.

"Can you surf in Guarujá? I'd really love to try surfing in Brazil one day," Amy said, eyes shining in a way that made his gut shift sideways.

"Do you surf?" He tried to keep the surprise out of his voice. Of course she did. She was from Florida.

"A little. A friend taught me a few years ago, so I like to at least watch."

The image of Amy in a white bikini paddling out into the surf next to him flickered on a screen in his head. He blinked it away. He would not be paddling out with anyone, much less Amy, who was here for less than three months.

She was so different from Halee, who'd

hated the ocean. The only way his ex had tolerated any bodies of water was if she was cruising down them on a yacht. They were such opposites he sometimes didn't know what they'd even seen in each other. Then again, he'd been a different person before the accident. Arrogant and far too sure of himself and his own immortality. A split-second collision on the field had taken care of that forever.

It seemed a lot of things had changed over the years. Including the type of woman he now found attractive?

His gaze collided with hers for a moment, before she smiled. "A day on the beach does sound fun."

It did actually. Roque couldn't remember the last time he took a day just to enjoy one of São Paulo's famous beaches. It had been a year or two.

"Great." It would also be nice to see his country through the eyes of a tourist. And hopefully it would help her as well. He took his phone out and scrolled through his work agenda. He didn't tend to take very many days off, so there were surgeries scattered through almost every day for the next several weeks, but he finally found an opening. "How about three weeks from Friday? I'll drive us out, rather than taking the bus."

"Should I bring a suit?" Amy asked.

"That's up to you, if you want to go in." Hell, he really hoped Amy would decide against that. He didn't need to go from imagining her wearing skimpy underthings to actually seeing her in swimwear, skimpy or not, although he had no idea why he was so leery of it. There were beautiful women everywhere in his country.

Just then the elevator doors opened. He glanced up and almost groaned aloud. It was his mom. And she was carrying a dry cleaner's bag. Inside of it, the teal color of Amy's long dress was clearly visible.

Amy also turned to look and her face quickly turned pink. Yep. Not the best scenario. And worse, his mother was striding toward them like a miniature powerhouse.

"I could have picked it up," Amy murmured to him.

"Yes, I told her that as well. But my *mamãe* does not always listen."

"*Roquinho, graças a Deus.* You are hard to locate in this place."

Roquinho? Really, Mother?

The diminutive form of his name meant Little Roque, and was one of her favorite ways to address him. It could be cute on occasion, but today wasn't one of those times.

"You could have had me paged. Or texted me."

"Oh, yes. I keep forgetting."

Her eyes zeroed in on Amy with a precision that would have made a surgeon proud. Any surgeon, except him. It brought back memories of their conversation about him meeting someone. The muscles in his gut tensed.

"This is her? The woman whose dress you almost ruined? Oh, the Fates…"

The way she said that made him close his eyes for a second or two. "Yes. Amy, this is my mother, Claudia Cardoza. Mom, this is Amy Woodell. She's here for the lecture series."

"Oh, yes, I know all about that."

Why did every word that came out of her

mouth sound like she was concocting some-thing? Something he knew he wouldn't like.

His mother handed him the dress and went up to Amy and put her hands on her shoulders, before pulling her close to deliver a resounding kiss on the cheek in true São Paulo fashion. In Rio it was customary to plant a kiss on both cheeks rather than just one, but in Brazil, people learned to adapt to where they were.

"It is very nice to kiss you, Amy."

Roque cringed at the misused English word. Especially since he'd had a thought or two about that recently himself.

"You mean nice to *meet* her, Mom."

His mom laughed and shrugged. While her English wasn't the best, her strong de-sire to be hospitable overrode her embar-rassment over mistakes. Most people found it charming.

So did he. Usually.

Amy spoke up. "Thank you for fixing my dress, Senhora Cardoza."

She said it in slow Portuguese that was perfect, if a little formal. His mom's eyes went wide and she threw him a nod that had a world of meaning to it.

Diabos! His mom's dislike of Halee had shown in her attitude and actions. And one of the biggest problems with his mother was that her emotions flashed across her face like a strobe light in a pitch-black room. She liked Amy. And, looking back, he could see how she had probably been right about his former fiancée, but that didn't mean she was right now. It was one of the reasons he'd never introduced her to any of his dates, although none of those had been anything more than casual dinners.

He liked his life the way it was. No entanglements. No demands on his time. A night here and there he could afford, but a lifetime of commitment? Nope. Not again. He'd been ready to marry Halee, until the accident happened and she dumped him. Maybe the next woman wouldn't have dumped him, but…

Gato escaldado tem medo de água fria.

Once bitten twice shy—wasn't that how they said it in English? In this case he liked the Portuguese version better.

"Roquinho said your, er, strap break? He step on it. Make it rip."

Amy smiled and replied in English. "It was an accident. Not a big deal. And thank you for fixing it. I would like to pay you for it."

His mom waved her hands. "No. No payment."

"But…"

"It is enough that Roque ask me for favor. He almost never ask. And now I ask favor in return. You come to dinner?"

"Dinner?"

"Yes. It would please me. Roque say your mother is from Brazil?"

"I, um…" Amy threw him a glance. "I would like that—if it is okay with Roque."

"Of course it is."

Great. His mom was suddenly making what should have been a small favor into something big and putting words in his mouth.

He fixed her with a look and responded in Portuguese, keeping his tone low. "Mamãe. Don't embarrass her."

All she did was smile and pat his cheek,

making him roll his eyes, suddenly very glad that he'd sent Lara and Peter to the nurse's desk.

"Find out a time that is good for her. She needs to see something besides this hospital. She will meet your father as well."

Why the hell was that even necessary? She didn't need to meet his father. Or any other family members, for that matter. But this was one argument he wanted to have in private.

"I will ask, but no promises."

Amy's quick grin came and went. So she hadn't missed the exchange, despite it being in Portuguese. Perfect. So not only was he going to help her find her uncle and go to a beach with her. Now she would be dining at his mother's house. A house with that big-screen television and plenty of baby pictures.

But the last thing he wanted to do was talk about why that wasn't a good idea. Or have someone bring up how he'd very nearly defrocked her in front of two hundred people. Or why he'd had a vivid dream last night in which she hadn't quite caught the dress before it slid to her feet—revealing her wearing lacy pink briefs and nothing else. He'd woken up in a puddle of sweat and need that he couldn't quite shake.

So, no. The less he thought about that night at the gala or her apartment—or the consequences of them—the better for everyone involved. So he kissed his mom and thanked her and said they needed to get back to work. She took the hint, but the smile she sent Amy said that she wasn't about to forget about this meeting. Or the dinner invitation.

All he could do was give an inward groan and hope that his mom let the subject of Amy and her dress drop.

Dress drop. Damn. There it was again.

He tightened his grip on the dress's hanger and determined that this was one subject he was not going to revisit. Or at least he would set that as his current goal, and hope against hope that he could kick that ball right past the goalkeeper and into the net.

CHAPTER FIVE

"AMY WOODELL—THIS IS ENZO DOS SANTOS and his wife, Lizbet."

Roque's dark eyes were on her as he made the introductions. More than three weeks had passed since his mom had appeared with her dress and the dinner invitation—which was scheduled to happen this evening after work.

The team had really started to sync, and Amy wasn't looking forward to being relegated to the physical therapy end of things, although she knew that was what had been planned all along.

Maybe *relegated* wasn't the right word for it, since Roque had told her about Enzo from the beginning. It seemed kind of funny to be meeting another person in his inner circle. First his mom—who'd given her a searching look that Amy hadn't quite been able to forget—and now his former coach. The man whose physical therapy she would be helping with once he had healed enough from his surgery.

"Nice to meet you both," she murmured.

Enzo's wife came forward and shook her hand, saying how grateful she was that Amy would be helping her husband recover. "Roque speaks very highly of you."

He did? Amy glowed with pride to think that perhaps Roque had enjoyed working with her as much as she had enjoyed working with him. And tonight she had dinner with his parents and tomorrow they were supposed to go on what Roque had called their field trip.

A phone call to a man named Abel Rodrigo had turned out to indeed be her uncle. Unfortunately, the visit they'd planned to make to him before going to the beach was going to have to be postponed, since her uncle was currently out of town on business. Maybe it was for the best, since she was already stressed about dining with Roque's parents and spending tomorrow at the beach with him.

Something that put her in an uneasy state of excitement, every time she thought about it. A whole day alone with him. Just her and Roque. Most of the last three weeks had been spent with the team, which she'd been glad of. At least, that's what she kept telling herself. Even though there'd been those odd moments when she sensed him looking at her. And she'd certainly glanced at him. More than once.

Lord. She needed to stop this.

Dragging her mind back to the patient, she forced herself to concentrate on what they were saying.

There was a kindness to Lizbet's manner that warmed Amy's heart. Despite that, there was something else—a spark of sadness, maybe?—in her eyes. Who could blame her? She and her husband had just gone through a terrible ordeal, one that wasn't over yet. Mr. Dos Santos owned one of the most famous football clubs in Rio. The same team Roque had once played for. He said they'd been friends for a very long time and it was obvious he cared for Enzo very much.

The man had almost lost his life to cancer. He'd certainly lost a good portion of his jaw. And now he was recovering from still more surgery. His lower mandible had been completely rebuilt. Enzo's jaws were immobilized at the moment, to allow the repairs to heal, so he had a whiteboard and marker to help him communicate. He was busy writing something and showing it to his wife.

She licked her lips, hesitating. "I, er, I don't know quite how to say this, but that doctor who tried to take over the surgery came to see Enzo again yesterday, under the guise of wanting to make sure he had everything he needed. Enzo doesn't care for him and would prefer he didn't have anything to do with his treatment."

Surely he wasn't talking about Dr. Carvalho. He was an excellent doctor from what she'd heard. "Which doctor was that?"

She handed the whiteboard back to her husband. "He introduced himself once, but he was kind of aggravating. He seems very concerned about Dr. Carvalho's involvement for no reason I can work out. After Enzo's recent difficulties..." Her voice trailed away. "I just don't want anything to set us back on a bad track. Things have been better since we've been in Brazil."

Enzo wrote something on his board and held it up.

She's worried. Felt I was depressed.

Amy could very well imagine he was. The man had been through a lot.

"I know who you're talking about," Roque said. "I'll see to it that he doesn't come see you again."

Wow. Roque could actually have another doctor banned from visiting a patient? Well, since Enzo was also his friend, it stood to reason that he would fight for him.

Was this who Roque meant when he said he wanted to be contacted if any doctor she didn't recognize tried to see Enzo? She was going to ask once they left the room.

Roque turned to her. "Amy, you've looked at Enzo's chart—do you want to give them an idea of how you'll go about physical therapy?"

"Sure." She went over the steps in her head. "First thing will be to pass your swallow test, which I don't anticipate you having any trouble doing."

Enzo nodded, writing something on his board. When he turned it toward her, the words were so unexpected they made her laugh.

If I don't cry, you're not doing your job.

"Well, I don't think I've ever had a patient that *wanted* me to make them cry before. But I assure you, you'll at least feel like crying at some point. I'll work you hard, but as long as you know my motivation is to meet our agreed-upon goals, then we'll do fine." She touched his hand. "I promise, I have the best of intentions and want us to work as a team."

The man relaxed back against his pillows, nodding and giving her a weak thumbs-up sign.

She couldn't imagine how hard it was for

this strong vibrant man to be laid up unable to work. Was that how Roque had felt after his injury?

She had no idea. What she did know, though, was that she was going to do her very best to get Enzo back on his feet and working again.

Roque smiled at his friends and said they'd let Enzo get some rest. She glanced at her phone. Almost four o'clock. They were supposed to be at Roque's parents' house at six.

A shiver went through her that she tried to suppress before he noticed it.

Walking through the door, she sucked down a quick breath and asked the first question that popped to her head. "Who was the doctor you were talking about? The one they don't want involved in Enzo's treatment? Do I need to know his name?"

He looked at her, dark eyes inscrutable, a lock of hair tumbling over his forehead before he dragged it back in place with a flick of his fingers. "Let's head to my office."

Walking down a hallway, she felt her belly tighten. In the time she'd been in Brazil she'd never been back to Roque's office. There'd never been any reason to. But it wasn't like he wanted to blurt a name out in the open where someone might overhear them. He reached a door with a placard listing his name and credentials. Pushing through it and motioning her inside, he closed it behind them. "Have a seat."

His voice had suddenly gone formal and cool. Or maybe that her imagination. Had she been wrong to ask him who the doctor was? But it wasn't blind curiosity. She wanted to be on guard if someone tried to upset her patient during physical therapy.

Her legs were suddenly a bit wobbly and she was glad to sit. Roque didn't go behind his desk; instead he leaned a hip on it. "Silvio Delgado."

"Sorry?"

"That's the doctor's name. I don't want him anywhere near Enzo. He tried to take the case from Dr. Simpson. Let's just say he was prevented from doing so."

"By you?"

"In part, but also by Dr. Carvalho and the administration. I won't go into the reasons for Delgado not being allowed near him. We'll just leave it at the fact that our patient doesn't like or trust him."

Our patient.

Had he actually said that? A feeling of warmth crashed over her, coursing through her veins and making her heart beat a little bit faster.

"I understand. Can you tell me what he looks like?"

One side of Roque's mouth went up in that devastating grin of his, making her mouth go completely dry.

"Let's just say you'll know who he is before you actually see him."

Why? Did he smell bad? Was he loud?

Ah, that was it. He was probably insufferable.

She was more and more sure that this was the snake that Flávia had been talking about during the welcome party. She'd meant to ask her who it was, but then figured it didn't really have anything to do with her, so she just forgot about it. Until now.

"Okay."

She relaxed back into the leather chair,

amazed at how comfortable it was. Actually, his whole office had a welcoming feel to it, which surprised her. She hadn't thought of Roque as a welcoming kind of guy, although that image was slowly shifting the more she got to know him. He was kind of dark with an intense, mesmerizing charm that she didn't quite understand. But she also caught glimpses of warmth in those dark eyes. Like a cup of cocoa that you wanted to savor for as long as possible.

And…making comparisons like that was not very smart. Even though he looked like heaven on earth perched over her like that.

"Okay, so I'll alert you if he shows up."

"Yes. Do." He paused. "And we need to talk about tonight. I don't want you to feel pressured into going."

"I don't, but if we need to postpone it I understand."

"No, I just wanted to give you a—how do you say it?—an out."

She sat up. "I'm not looking for an out. Unless you'd rather I not come."

"My *mamãe* can be rather direct with her requests."

"Kind of like her son?" He'd been pretty direct about not wanting her to go to the beach on her own.

There went that grin again. "You think I'm direct?"

"Aren't you?"

"Maybe." He tilted his head. "But only when speaking from one doctor to another."

He'd evidently misunderstood what she was talking about. "I'm not a doctor."

"No. But I have a feeling you will be. Someday. Why did you never pursue your doctorate in physical therapy?"

That was a hard question. Her mom had been on her own for a very long time, and had helped Amy as much as she could during her years in college. Amy hadn't thought it fair that she continue her studies on her mom's dime.

"It's complicated. But I'm thinking of going back to school to get it once I get home. There are just never enough hours in a day."

"I know that feeling. Okay. So, tonight is set. And about tomorrow. Are you still wishing to go?"

Wishing? Probably more than she should.

"I am, if it's okay with you. Although I really don't mind going by myself, if you have too many things you need to take care of."

"No. I said I would take you, and I try to always keep my word."

Making it sound like he wasn't looking forward to it at all. And how did she feel about going with him without the side trip to her uncle's house?

Excited. And that scared her. Weeks were starting to fly by, and that wild, sexy fling she'd envisioned having with some man while she was here hadn't happened. There wasn't even a single prospect. By the time she finished work each day, she was too tired to feel lonely. And going to a bar by herself looking for a likely prospect seemed kind of pitiful and not very safe. Here or in the United States. There was always Krysta and Flávia, except she'd heard the venom specialist was traveling back and forth to the Atlantic Forest region of Brazil, and she'd only seen Krysta in passing, although she had suggested the pair of them meet up for a dinner or a shopping trip sometime.

"Do you want to surf or swim tomorrow?"

He'd said taking a suit was up to her, but she'd already decided against it. And there was a tension in his voice that said she'd made the right choice.

"I think I'd just like to sightsee this time, if that's okay." She was already in a state about going with him. She didn't need to throw a bathing suit and water into the mix. And although water could conceal a whole lot of what happened below its surface, if she were going to have that fling, she'd rather it be in complete privacy.

Was she actually considering Roque for the position?

No, of course not, although Roque hadn't mentioned a girlfriend, and the blonde from the soiree had never reappeared.

"That's fine. We can see more that way. We'll just walk on the sand."

She smiled. A walk on the beach with him sounded very, very nice. Too nice, in fact. "I don't want to fill your car with the stuff."

"It's seen worse." He shifted his cane, pushing it a little to the left. "How do you feel speaking in Portuguese when it's just you and me?"

Just you and me.

Her toes tingled at the sound of that, the sensation spreading up her calves and tickling her thighs. She loved hearing him speak in his native tongue. Maybe a little too much. "I—I'm not the best at it, but I can try."

Great. Now she was stammering, even in English.

"I think it would be an asset for your work. You said you live in South Florida. Isn't there a large community of Brazilians there?"

There was. She'd had a couple of patients who were Brazilians actually, and Amy had practiced tae kwon do at her local *dojang* with a Brazilian instructor. Marcos had sent a couple of people injured at tournaments to physical therapy and had offered to "hire" her if she ever needed a little extra work. She'd gotten the feeling that the interest went beyond pupil/instructor relationship, but she hadn't wanted things to get messy and ruin their professional relationship. And she'd been pretty wary of getting involved with men back then.

Maybe she should remember that decision and treat her relationship with Roque the same way. If she were smart, she'd call off the beach trip. And dinner with his folks. Except she wanted to go to both. More than she should. But she was only here in Brazil for a couple more months, so how messy could it get in that period of time?

Pretty damned messy, if she wasn't careful.

But right now it wasn't, and he wanted to start speaking in Portuguese.

She swallowed.

"You're right. There is a large population of Brazilians there. So I probably should practice."

"We can start by using the language on our beach trip, and I will correct you when you make a mistake. How's that? It will also make you look less like a tourist if we're not speaking English."

Ah, now she got the reason for it. It would make them less of a target for thieves while at Guarujá. "That makes sense."

It would be awkward, since she "knew" Roque in English. Speaking Portuguese with him would seem intimate, even though she knew he didn't mean it that way.

And she knew her mom in two languages, so how was that any different? Maybe it wasn't, except Amy had never been required to respond in Portuguese. She'd just needed to understand what was said.

"I see worry on your face. Don't be scared. I think it will become easier with practice. And you'll find I am a very forgiving coach."

She bit her lip as the tingling spread to places far higher than her calves.

The image of him "coaching" her in hoarse tones as they practiced things other than Portuguese trickled through her subconscious, becoming a torrent as each mental picture became more explicit than the last.

Oh, God. Time to move this conversation to something else.

"Speaking of coaches. Do you miss playing football?"

Ugh! "Something else" did *not* mean reminding him of a time in his life that was probably painful.

"Or shouldn't I ask?"

"It's okay." His fingers, as if on automatic pilot, found his cane and fingered the handle. "Yes, I miss some things about it. But not others. I miss having a leg that is whole more than I miss the game."

Whole? Did he really think that?

"Your leg *is* whole. It's just a different kind of whole. It's a part of what makes you…you."

"A different kind of whole? I'm not sure I agree with that. I live in this body, I know what it feels."

From her Google search—and yes, she was ashamed to admit that she'd done more of her share of reading up on him—he'd been very good at what he did. Had been one of his team's top players, in fact.

"It's just your normal. People are not cookie cutter shapes. Everyone has their own strengths and weaknesses."

"Cookie cutter."

"It means people are not exactly alike."

He smiled, and the act warmed any chilliness that had gathered in his expression. "No. People are not just alike. And that is a good thing, I think."

"Yes, it is." Roque was like no one she'd ever met.

His hand had moved away from his cane and was now gripping the edge of his desk beside his left thigh.

A very strong-looking thigh.

She struggled to think of something to say that would stop her train of thought, which was starting to barrel into dangerous territory. "I heard Peter mention missing his wife and kids today."

"It is natural. You don't have someone at home that you miss?"

The sad thing was, she didn't. She had no serious relationship; she wasn't even dating. And although she had friends at the hospital and at the rehab center, she didn't hang out with them as much as she might expect. Many of them were married with families and, like Peter, all they wanted to do was get home to them. More and more, she'd been thinking of what Roque had said about getting her doctorate. She'd put it off as something to do later. But what if later never came and she looked back with regret. Maybe it was a time to make a promise to herself.

"No one special, but that's okay. Especially since I'm going to apply for the doctorate program as soon as I get home."

And just like that, the decision she'd been toying with for some time was made.

The hand that had been gripping his desk relaxed a little. Was he worried that she might be interested in him…in staying because of him?

The brakes on that train screeched as she applied them hard, the engine struggling to stop, the boxcars she'd added over the last couple of weeks piling up behind it.

"I'm glad you are. The Achilles' tendon patient liked what you had to say. And it would give you opportunities to teach at universities."

She'd thought the same thing. If she ever got to a place that she didn't have the strength she needed to manipulate patients the way they needed to be, it would give her options. And although she hadn't been intimately involved with that first patient's surgery she'd observed at Paulista, she had been at his appointments and observed his rehab. She was due to go again in a few days as a matter of fact.

"Yes, that's what I thought as well." She tilted her head. "When is Mr. Dos Santos going to start physical therapy?"

"In a couple of weeks. The repairs are stable and he's due for his swallow test tomorrow."

The day they'd be at the beach. "You don't want to be here for him? I'll understand if we have to put off our trip."

"His wife will be there, and I'll check on him when we get back. I think the last thing Enzo wants are for twenty people to be gathered around to watch him. He's a pretty determined guy. I don't doubt he'll pass with flying colors, which is a good thing with where his mind has been lately. I know. I've been there."

Was he talking about what Enzo had written about his depression? Well, Roque had had a right to be depressed, if so. He'd been a brilliant young soccer player, and in the blink of an eye everything he'd worked so hard for had been taken from him.

"Sometimes things work out the way they should. You do brilliant work here at the hospital." She nodded at his left leg. "Would you be at Paulista if you hadn't been injured?"

"Probably not. I'm old enough now that my career would be pretty much over, and I'd probably be coaching or stuck at a desk job somewhere." He sighed. "That doesn't mean the road from there to here was easy. It took ten long years of school to become a doctor."

"No. I'm sure it wasn't. But where are you more needed at this point in your life?"

He laughed. "You have a way of turning things around to look at their best side."

"The dangers of being a physical therapist. We're trained to be positive and optimistic. It's a good way to motivate our patients."

"I think those characteristics come naturally to you."

Did they? She didn't always feel all that optimistic. She just needed to be "up" for her patients. Needed to be a motivator when they came in feeling life would never be the same, ever again.

The exact way Roque had probably felt when told his career as a football player was over. "Thanks, but I'm not sure that's true. It's just part of my job description. You mentioned being a coach. That never appealed to you?"

"No. I thought about it once or twice, but didn't see myself doing that. Not with my old team, anyway."

"It would have been too hard to watch them play while you felt sidelined?" The way he'd said the words gave her pause.

"That would have been hard, yes, but my reasons were more...personal."

Personal? He and the team's owner seemed to get along great; he'd even confided in Roque about that other oncologist, Dr. Delgardo. So she didn't see that "personal" reason arising there. But if he wanted her to know, he would tell her, so that was her signal to leave it alone.

Oh! Roque had been engaged to an actress, according to her search. Who was now married to a player on his former team. Of course he wouldn't want to see her day in and day out. That made perfect sense.

Her heart cramped. Surely it was better to know what a person was like before getting married to them. She could certainly thank her lucky stars now that her boyfriend had dumped her *before* marriage rather than after. Although she'd been gutted at the time.

"Things have a way of showing you a person's true colors." In case he didn't know that expression, she added, "Of seeing them for who they really are. Like your accident. When your soccer days came to an end, it revealed who you really are."

"Interesting." His smile was slow and unbearably sexy. "And who am I...really?"

The ground had suddenly gotten shaky under her feet. Why had she said that? "You're a man who cares about his patients and his friends, and who likes to keep his word."

There! That was the least personal thing she could think of to say. And they were both true.

He got to his feet. "But you could say that about almost every doctor here at Paulista."

"But we're not talking about every doctor." She was suddenly having a hard time catching her breath. "We're talking about you."

Thinking he was ready to shoo her out of his office, she climbed to her feet as well. Big mistake. Because it set her right in front of him. Close enough to catch the warm musky scent of his aftershave. To see the slight dusting of stubble across his chin. And those lips that seemed to capture her attention time and time again…

Roque made no effort to move away. "So we were. So let's talk about you. Do you want to know how I see *you*?"

She wasn't sure she did, but it was as if her mouth was controlled by forces outside of her body. "Yes."

He touched a finger to her jawline. "I see a woman in a teal dress that's an inch or two too long for her. A woman who didn't let that stop her from coming to the party." He'd switched to Portuguese, and she stood there transfixed by his touch and his voice as he continued. "I saw bits and pieces of you in that patient file you included in your application to the program. And the real you made me very glad I said yes to you being in the program."

He dropped his hand, but continued to meet her eyes. "You want what's best for your patients and those around you."

"I'm not as saintly as you make me sound."

"Aren't you?" His gaze trailed down her neck. "You're like a marble sculpture that stands in front of a church."

If he could read her thoughts right now, he might change his mind. Her pulse pounded in her head, mouth going dry as she stared back at him. "Sculptures aren't real. I assure you, I am flesh and blood. Just like you."

"Are you?" One hand slid into her hair and cupped her nape, his thumb just behind the tender skin of her ear. But that wasn't what made her take another step in his direction. That came from somewhere inside of her, from the part that wanted to know what it would be like to be kissed by him, to feel herself pressed against him. She could damn herself later, but for right now...

He looked into her eyes, maybe seeing

the jumble of emotions boiling just under the surface. Then his head started a slow descent, until it was just her and him. And his lips on hers.

CHAPTER SIX

ROQUE HAD NEVER felt anything so sweet. Or so undeniably sexy. The second his mouth touched those silky soft lips of hers, Amy's arms wound around his neck.

And it was heaven.

She'd said she was no saint. But neither was he. He'd proven that time and time again when one date didn't lead to another. But right here, right now, there was nowhere else he'd rather be.

His tongue eased into her mouth and found a moist heat that set his body on fire. One arm circled her back, and he leaned his weight against his desk for stability. The last thing he wanted to do right now was fall. Or lose contact with her. And damn if she somehow didn't wind up between his splayed legs and pressed against the part of him that had dreamed of this happening ever since he stepped on her dress a month ago.

And now here he was.

Right where he shouldn't be, for so many reasons.

She was a visitor at his hospital. And she was only here for three months.

Maybe it was the latter point that kept him in place.

Amy made a sound in her throat, her hips inching forward and back in a way she probably wasn't even aware of. But he was. He felt every little movement. A vision of his desk and her on it came to mind. That image lingered, toying with different angles and positions.

But before he could even think about turning them so that she was against the desk instead of him, the phone on his hip buzzed, the noise breaking into the silent struggle that was going on between them.

Amy froze for a second. Then she jerked back, her arms releasing their hold on him.

She kept moving until she was against the chair, and no doubt if that hadn't been there she would have kept going until she was out the door. One of her hands grabbed the armrest and the other pressed against her mouth.

Hell, what had he been thinking? He hadn't been.

When she finally spoke, she said, "I am so sorry. I don't know what... I have no idea why..."

He knew why. All too well. And it wasn't her fault, it was his. "Don't. I let things get out of hand. There's no excuse I can give."

"I was a willing participant. You would have known quickly enough if I hadn't been."

That made him laugh, despite the regret that was coursing through him at his behavior. "Really? What would you have done?"

"Put you on the ground."

"Ah, that's right. You know tae kwon do."

"I do. I have a first-degree black belt in it."

His eyes widened. "That shouldn't surprise me."

"But it does? Well, you can thank my mom. She's the one who insisted that I go for lessons. She wanted me to be able to defend myself."

"It sounds like you can."

Roque glanced at his watch, surprised to see it was almost five. "About dinner…"

"Let me guess. You don't want me to go now."

Something passed through her eyes. Like she was expecting him to cancel on her.

"No, I was going to ask if you needed to go home to change first, because we'll be cutting it close, if so."

What looked like relief passed through her eyes. "So you still want me to come?"

"Is there a reason I shouldn't?"

She smiled. "Evidently not. You're very good at compartmentalizing, you know that?"

"At what?"

"Putting everything into separate boxes in your mind."

He was actually. Partly the result of his accident and what had happened with Halee, and partly because of his job. "This is one thing I will not hide away in a box. That way I can make sure it won't happen again."

"I can help with that. Remember that whole 'on the ground' thing?" She let go of the arm of the chair as if having regained her composure.

His smile widened, relieved that she wasn't going to blow this all out of proportion.

"You would use some of your moves on me?" And just like that, Roque was back in a different frame of mind, going over that kiss blow by blow.

"You don't want to find out."

The problem was… He did. But if he was going to get through this dinner intact, he was going to have to keep his head. Because his mother was very, very shrewd. And the last thing he needed was for her to guess what he and Amy had been doing in this office.

Otherwise she'd be on the phone with her priest and reserving the church.

That wasn't going to happen.

If he could just remember that Amy was here for just a few months and that she had her heart set on earning her doctorate in the States, he would be fine.

He didn't want another relationship. And the last thing he wanted was to keep anyone from their dreams.

Claudia and Andre Cardoza welcomed her into the cookout area of their little getaway house with the same warmth his mom had displayed at the hospital.

"Thank you so much for inviting me."

They'd opted to host the meal outside of the crush of São Paulo, instead of at the family home. Roque said it was because his dad—a police officer—liked to get away from town on the weekends, whenever he could.

"We are glad Roque brought you." Andre was the spitting image of his son, although his dark hair was peppered with gray. With a skewer loaded with some type of meat in one hand and a brick grill behind him, he looked totally in his element.

Unlike Roque, who seemed ill at ease. Well, that made two of them. She'd actually been surprised that he wanted her to come, and maybe it would have been easier if they'd canceled their plans, but Amy had truly liked Claudia and would have hated for her to go to the trouble of fixing her a meal only to have her not show up.

His mom brought her a bottle of water. "Please help yourself to anything. Dinner won't be long. Roque, why don't you show her around."

"Okay."

He grabbed a water for himself and motioned her to follow him. The walled-in compound was alive with flowers and greenery, and there were several hammocks scattered throughout the space. A clay-tiled building was to the left, and must be where they slept when they weren't outside. It was kind of like a cabin they might have back home in Florida. Without the sand.

"What's the Portuguese word for this kind of place again?"

"It's a *chácara*. Kind of like a country home. Only not."

He could say that again. When she thought of a country home, she thought of a white stucco home with a wraparound porch. This was more like a campground. One they had all to themselves. It was charming, and under other circumstances she might have found it heavenly.

Except she was hyperaware of every move Roque made. Of his broad shoulders and narrow waist and the way he had felt against her.

He'd been attracted to her, that much was obvious. She'd felt the very real evidence of that.

And despite her talk about compartmentalizing, it was not going to be easy to lock that particular memory into a box and keep it there.

But somehow she was going to have to do just that.

A fling? With Roque?

Just hours earlier, she'd entertained that exact thought. Until she realized just how deadly his kiss was to her senses.

"How long have your parents owned this?"

"Actually, this was passed down to them by my grandparents, who built it many years ago."

A pond nestled against one corner of the property, the greenery behind it camouflaging the protective wall that kept intruders out. "Does it have electricity?"

"It does now. It didn't originally." He grinned. "They also added plumbing a few years ago."

"I bet that makes life a lot more comfortable."

He motioned to one of the chairs that flanked the body of water. "When I was a kid, I didn't seem to think about what this place lacked. I just liked being with family."

Since the only family Amy had had around had been her mom and dad—her grandparents had passed away before she was born—it was a little hard to imagine family get-togethers that involved more than just the three of them. She sank into one of the wrought-iron chairs with a sigh. "It's beautiful. Serene."

And suddenly she was glad she'd come. This place might be the perfect bridge to transport her from her heightened emotional state to a place that was more tranquil. At least she could hope. The pond boasted a small rock waterfall that had to be powered by a pump, although she couldn't see it.

"Yes. My father's job is very difficult. This helps him put things into perspective. To realize that life is more than fighting drug lords in *favelas*."

Some of the slums of Brazil were known for being controlled by different gangs, going as far as limiting who entered and left the community. "I can't imagine how hard that must be."

"I grew up knowing that my father could go to work one day and never make it home. I think that's why the Chácara do Cardoza is so important to him. He's had offers on the property, but he always turns them down."

"You'll inherit this someday, then."

"I imagine."

There was something in his voice. "You don't want it?"

"At one time, I would have said no. But that was a long time ago." He stretched his leg in front of him, propping his cane against his thigh.

"Is it bothering you?"

"No."

The answer was curt, like it was whenever she asked about his leg. He didn't like talking about it. She could understand that. No one liked to admit to having a weakness.

"Sorry."

He tipped his head back so that it leaned against the high back of the chair, then turned to look at her. "It is I who am sorry. My leg is tired from the day, but it will be fine tomorrow."

For their trip to the beach. They would have a lot of walking, from what he'd said. But it would be better for his muscles than standing in one spot doing surgeries like he probably did day in and day out. She'd been tempted to back out of their trip, but she also didn't want Roque to know how much that kiss had affected her.

"What should I bring?"

"To the beach?" He paused. "Probably the same things you would take in Florida. Sunscreen, maybe a hat. Shoes that are easy to walk in and remove sand from."

"Okay. Do you want me to meet you somewhere?"

"I think it would be better if I picked you up in front of the Fonte Cristalina. Say at nine o'clock in the morning?"

CHAPTER SEVEN

WHY ON EARTH had she told him to meet her in front of her apartment complex? Or agreed to come with him at all? Was she crazy? She was already affected by him in ways she didn't want to think about, and now she was going to spend the day with him. Alone.

She'd gotten outside ten minutes early so he wouldn't have to wait, and in that short period of time several people had come out, commenting on her hat and the straw bag containing her sunscreen. She'd been able to repeat that she was going to the beach. One woman had asked if she wanted company! Which had gotten super awkward when she said she'd been invited by the doctor she was working with.

But it might have been more awkward if

It was already past eight, but Amy was in no hurry to get back to her apartment. Maybe because she knew that once that happened, she was going to dissect every single second of her time in his office and figure out how what had started out as a completely professional conversation had gone so totally off the rails.

"That sounds like a plan."

A half hour later, Amy was sitting outside at a large farmhouse-style table laughing at stories that Andre shared about some of his most embarrassing moments as a police officer. She was pretty sure he'd also experienced some awful moments as well. A couple of times Claudia had reached across and squeezed her hand, smiling at her and asking if Amy wanted this or that and encouraging her to eat another bite of the delicious grilled meat that was so common in Brazil.

"I'm very...*satisfeita*." One of her mother's favorite words surfaced without warning, and she swallowed hard, hoping no one realized she was choked with grief—a grief she thought she'd worked through.

Roque peered at her through the growing shadows. "Are you okay?"

"Yes. Just enjoying the evening."

And she was, much to her surprise. A little too much, maybe. That's probably where that little burst of emotion had come from. Thinking about how her mom would have loved sharing this moment with her.

But they'd had plenty of other happy times. And she treasured each of them.

Roque glanced at his watch. "Well, I know you and Dad are spending the night here, but I need to get Amy back to her apartment. It's been a long day."

Claudia stood up and came around and kissed her son on the cheek and then turned to Amy and hugged her tight. *"Venha de novo, ta?"*

"I will. Thank you so much." As much as she appreciated Claudia's encouragement to return to visit, she very much doubted she would ever see Roque's parents again.

Hopefully her smile hid any sadness she might feel over that fact. But the reality was, these three months would soon be little more than a tiny moment in time. So she commit-

ted as much of this place and their faces as she could to memory.

And maybe one day she would be able to draw those memories back up and remember them with a smile that was a little more genuine than the one currently plastered to her face.

At least she hoped so.

there were suddenly five people cramming into Roque's car.

Finally he arrived, and she jumped in and slammed her door, giving him the biggest brightest smile she could manage, hoping that he wouldn't guess how nervous she was. "Ready? Let's go."

He glanced at her with a frown. "What's the big rush?"

"Well, the explanations have been a little difficult."

"Why?"

The single word summed it up brilliantly. Why was it a problem? She was the one who was fumbling around and making it a bigger deal than it was. Somehow dinner with Roque's parents had been easier than this beach outing was proving to be, and she wasn't sure why. Maybe it was that whole thing of him wanting to speak Portuguese when they were alone. So far, she was not following that course, since the words pouring from her mouth were all in English.

"I don't know. I think it just feels…" She couldn't come up with the right word to save her life.

"After yesterday, do you mean?"

"Yes." As usual, he'd hit the nail on the head. If she could somehow stop overanalyzing every aspect of what had happened in his office, maybe she could put it all behind her.

"No one knows about that except us. So our outing will only appear strange to others, if we make it that way."

Which is exactly what she'd done. Maybe because she couldn't just hide her feelings the way others might. Even Roque kept his emotions tucked well out of sight. Except for yesterday.

But had that been due to an overflow of feelings? Or simply because they were a man and woman who were attracted to each other physically?

"You're right, of course. There's no reason to feel guilty. I'm just one of those people who ends up getting caught red-handed if I do something wrong."

"Well, our hands are not red, because no one saw us."

Amy laughed. "That's one way of putting it." She loved the way he used expressions with confidence even if he didn't quite understand the meaning.

With that he started the car and pulled away from the curb. "Are you looking forward to seeing Guarujá? If you brought a towel, we can sit on the beach for a while."

"Sounds great. Have you ever been to Caraguatatuba? Apparently there's a great surfing beach there? Do you know it?"

"Massaguaçu. The surf is not always consistent, but it can get busy at peak times of the year. If you decide to go surfing there, take a buddy."

It's not like she'd be in Brazil long enough to do that or had anyone to do it with. "I'll keep that in mind."

His fingers tightened on the wheel, and he turned to look at her. "Seriously. The riptides can be deadly."

"I won't go alone. I promise."

"Good."

An hour and a half later, they were in Guarujá, and Amy couldn't hold back a gasp. It was almost intimidating, with row after row of pristine condominiums. Nothing like the Chácara do Cardoza from last night.

Traffic was heavy, but not as bad as at the center of São Paulo, which many times saw bumper-to-bumper traffic and motorcycles that whizzed frantically between the rows of cars.

"Are you okay?"

"Yes, just didn't expect it to look like this honestly. There must be thousands of people living here."

Roque smiled. "Hundreds of thousands. And I was right."

"Right? About what?"

"I do like seeing this place through the eyes of a tourist."

So he hadn't brought anyone here during previous years' lecture programs? If what he said was true, it appeared not.

She couldn't stop a smile as a wave of warmth poured over her. "I'll try not to disappoint you."

"You have not disappointed, Amy. Believe me."

Something about the way he said that sent a shiver over her.

He's not talking about that kiss, Amy.

More likely he was talking about how she did her job at the hospital.

Roque found a paid parking garage and slid his car into the first available spot, taking his ticket and paying the attendant.

Scooping her beach bag from the back seat, she crossed the strap of her purse over her chest and kept the wicker tote containing her beach gear in her hand.

"Do you want me to carry something?"

She glanced at his hands, noting he'd brought nothing with him. "I'm good. It's not heavy. I just have a towel and sunscreen in there." She dropped her sunglasses over her nose to help cut the glare from the sun, which was already warm.

Skirting one of the large apartment blocks, they arrived on a long sandy strip that led down to the water. On it was a sea of red striped umbrellas that stretched as far as the eye could see. "Wow, they're all dressed up for company, aren't they?"

"It's pretty impressive, I agree." He glanced at one of the nearby buildings. "Why don't you keep going, and I'll catch up with you in a minute."

She looked over at where his attention had gone, but saw nothing, so she did as he'd asked and started across the sand. She then took off her shoes and stuffed them into her bag, enjoying the warmth beneath her bare feet.

Less than a minute later, she felt a slight tug on her bag. The hair raised on the back of her neck when she sensed someone directly behind her.

Roque had been right.

When the bump happened again, she instinctively whirled around, hooking her foot around the calf of the pickpocket and yanked as hard as she could, sending him flying to the ground.

Only at the deep "oomph" did she realize her mistake.

Roque lay sprawled across the sand, his cane about three feet to his right. "Oh, God, I'm sorry. I thought someone was trying to steal something from my bag."

He propped himself up with his hands

on the sand. "I guess you really can defend yourself."

"Of course I can. I already told you I know tae kwon do." She frowned. "Wait. What do you mean, I can defend myself? Were you *trying* get a reaction from me?"

"I thought I'd see how aware you were of your surroundings." He reached for his cane. "Very, evidently."

"It was pure instinct. Are you hurt? Your leg?"

Pushing off with his cane, he shook his head and tried to get to his feet, only to have his walking aid sink into the soft sand, leaving him stranded on the ground. "My pride is the only casualty, it seems."

She reached down to help him up, and he let her, managing to heft himself to his feet. "This feels like reversed roles. I did the same for you, when your dress was ripped and you couldn't get out of my car. Remember?"

Only too well. "Yes, well, at least you didn't step on my dress on purpose. Unlike me, who purposely tripped you."

He squeezed her hand for a minute before releasing it, leaning against her as he tried to get his cane situated. "But I did reach into your bag on purpose, just now, so you did the right thing."

He took a step, and the color suddenly drained from his face. He stopped in place.

"You *are* hurt. I am so, so sorry!"

"It's nothing." He reached down to massage his left thigh. "Just a muscle cramp. I get them sometimes when the nerves misfire."

She turned and faced him. This was her chance. "I can help with that."

"No, you can't."

There was a darkness to his voice that was at odds with the reality of the situation. She actually could help. If he'd let her.

She took a deep breath and let it out in a controlled hiss, trying to keep herself from taking his refusal personally. "I can't make your injury go away, but I can help with the pain you have right now."

"I've tried it."

She tilted her head. "And it didn't help at all? I find that hard to believe. I can do a deep tissue massage that—"

"Absolutely not."

This time, she let the anger come to the forefront. "Are you kidding me? You said you liked how I treated Bobby Sellers, said it showed I could think outside of the box, and now you're acting like I have nothing to offer."

She'd lived through this hot and cold nonsense before and wasn't about to put up with it from him.

"I did not say that."

"Not in so many words, but you implied it. Please let me try. If it doesn't help, you've lost nothing. But if it does…"

"You won't always be here, Amy, so it's better if I don't get used to any—"

"Damn it! You're the one who told me Paulista is an amalgamation of all the best hospitals in the world. There are other therapists you could go to if it turns out this works. I let your mother fix my dress. Let me try to help your leg."

"What would you do?"

He leaned on the cane with both hands. It must really hurt. She'd never seen him this vulnerable before. "I'll use essential oils in a carrier oil and massage them into your skin.

The heat generated from my hands will help the oils absorb."

"And if it doesn't help? Will you then stop suggesting I seek therapy?"

She blinked. He was going to let her try? She'd somehow expected a bigger fight than that. While a part of her was relieved, another part was worried that maybe he knew something she didn't. Something that would prove her wrong. "Are you sure it's just a muscle cramp? Could you have landed wrong and damaged something else?" She'd hooked his right leg, not the injured one, but anything could have happened as he went down.

"It's not dislocated or broken, if that's what you mean. I recognize this pain. It's just muscle."

"Can you make it back to the car?"

"I can finish our tour." But when he tried to take another step, he winced and stopped again.

"No, you can't. Give me your cane."

"I don't think—"

She jerked it from beneath his hands and hooked it over her beach bag.

"What the hell, Amy?"

She moved to his affected side. "Put your arm around me."

"No."

"What's wrong, Roque? Scared? Of little ole me?"

"I am not scared."

He might not be, but she was now wondering about the wisdom of asking him to touch her, even as an offer of help.

Surprisingly, he put his arm around her waist while she jammed her shoulder under his arm, and the second he did, a sense of rightness came over her, the warm solidness of his body fitting perfectly against hers. The side of her breast nestled against his chest in a way that made her nipples tighten at the slightest hint of friction. She held perfectly still and willed it away. It didn't work.

Oh, no. Not what she wanted. At all.

She hesitated, tearing her mind apart for some other way to get him to the car and coming up blank. Maybe this was why he hadn't wanted her helping him. Because he knew how he made her feel.

Not the time to be thinking about any of this, Amy.

"Let's go. Lean on me as we walk."

Slowly they made their way back to the sidewalk and soon all thoughts of how he made her body react vanished. Roque didn't make a sound, but when she glanced up at his face, his mouth was bracketed with white lines of pain. Why had she swept his leg out from under him?

Because she'd honestly thought someone was trying to steal something from her bag, and pure instinct had taken over. He said the pain was muscular. Well, she would know as soon as she laid her hands on his skin. Either the muscles would be knotted and hard or she'd realize something else was wrong.

Lord, she hoped he was right. She didn't think he'd like having to postpone all his surgeries because of something as stupid as a case of mistaken identity.

Well, they would worry about that when the time came.

"Do you have your international driver's license?"

"Yes, do you need me to drive?"

He leaned more of his weight on her and another warning shimmy went through her stomach, bringing back all the uneasy sensations she thought she'd banished. Evidently not.

His skin was warm against her. So alive. So—

"Maybe. If you can drive a manual transmission."

He's hurt, Amy, why are you even thinking along these lines?

She responded carefully. "My car at home is actually a stick shift. We don't have quite this much traffic, though, except for when the snowbirds come to town."

"Snowbirds?"

"It's what we call people from the north when they come to Florida to get away from their winter weather."

"Country homes? Like what my parents have?"

She smiled. "Not quite, but maybe the same idea."

Fifteen minutes later, they made it to his car, and Amy helped him get inside, lifting his injured leg and sliding it onto the floor gently. The muscles of his calf were firm, no hint of atrophy from babying his leg. She drew in a deep breath. This was a man who would not baby anything. So if he was letting her do this...

He said something she didn't quite catch before muttering, "I feel like a...an...*idiota*."

That word came through in any language. "Stop it. And get ready to hang on." She then sent him a smile that she hoped was full of mischief. If she could distract him, maybe that would interfere with his body's pain receptors. She'd heard of it working.

"Maybe I should drive."

"If what I'm seeing on your face is any indication of your pain levels, then putting you behind the wheel would be even more dangerous than my mad car skills."

He leaned his head against the headrest. "I do not even want to know what 'mad car skills' means."

"Probably just as well. Okay, here we go."

She stowed her gear in the back and then climbed into the driver's seat, adjusting it to her shorter stature. Roque handed her the keys.

Getting the car started, she managed to back out of the slot and drive up the ramp that led out of the parking garage. "Anything I need to do?" Besides take note of every move the man made?

"No. I already included a tip when I paid."

"Do you have a GPS? If not, you'll have to give me some instructions on how to get to your place." One of her biggest failings was that if she wasn't driving, she didn't pay attention to the route when she was a passenger. She'd tried to correct that trait time and time again, but she either got caught up in the conversation or the scenery.

"I'll put it on my phone. You'll just basically take the Immigrantes Highway all the way back to São Paulo."

"Sorry. That means nothing to me."

"Here." He pushed a button and a voice came out of the phone. It was in Portuguese, so it took a moment or two for Amy to adjust to the computer-generated speech. "Don't worry, I'll help. My leg feels better now that it's not having to support my weight."

Now that her insistence had gotten her what she wanted, she was starting to wonder

how smart she'd been in making that offer.
Except she was the one who'd caused his
pain. The least she could do was try to fix it.

Her heart clenched and she knew she
was in trouble with this man. Not that she
was going to let herself fall in love with
him. She'd meant it when she said she was
going back to start her doctoral studies. She
couldn't do that in Brazil.

And Roque's life was here. In Brazil.
Wrapped up in his work and the life he was
living. Just because she liked the way his
body felt against hers changed nothing.

The fact that she did meant she'd have to
be even more careful. That kiss had sent her
senses spiraling toward treacherous territory. If his phone hadn't buzzed…

Yes. That phone. A lifesaver for sure.

There was no room in her life for the long
leather sofa she'd seen in his office. And as
she'd left the office, her eyes had somehow
caught and taken note of the fact that there
was a lock on the door.

All they'd have to do was turn the little
latch and—

Ridiculous. She needed to stop this!

The GPS said something and she forced her mind back to her driving and getting them home. "Do you live in the same part of town as I do?"

"About five miles before you get there. It's a red-tiled building."

"Tell me when we're getting close, so I can start looking."

For the next twenty minutes or so, he sat in silence, eyes closed tight. She wasn't sure if he'd fallen asleep or if he was in so much pain that he was just trying to cope.

Suddenly he straightened up, glancing at her. "Not much farther."

"On this road?"

"Yes, two blocks ahead on your right. Condomínio Apollo. Just pull into the lower level garage. The numbers are painted on the spaces. I'm 601."

She found his building, and shifting the vehicle into a lower gear, she managed the sharp curving turn that led into what looked like a maze. But the numbers were laid out in order and she found his spot down another line of spaces to the left. Fortunately, most of the tenants were at work so she could navigate fairly easily. Otherwise she might have had to make a couple of three-point turns.

She glanced at him. "Any better at all?"

"I guess we'll find out." His jaw was tight, but that might be from anticipated pain rather than actual current pain.

"I'll come around and help." She put his keys in the pocket of her sundress, retrieved her purse and beach bag, in case she needed to catch a taxi back to her own apartment, and went around to the passenger side door. Opening it, she said, "Give me your hands."

"Let me have my cane, and I'll see if I can manage."

Without a word she got his walking stick, but instead of handing it to him she draped it over her arm. "Take. My. Hands."

"Amy…"

She got down on her haunches next to the low-slung car and looked him in the eye. "Trust me, Roque. Please. The less strain you put on those muscles right now, the more likely we'll be able to massage the knots out of them."

"*Merde.*"

The swear word was so soft she almost

missed it. Her heart ached for him in a way that it didn't for most of the cases she'd worked on. She'd learned early on that if she could harden that traitorous organ it was better for her patients, because she had to push them to help them heal. And it was often painful. She'd had strong, strapping men cry in her presence and had to promise she'd tell no one.

She stood and took his hands in hers and gave them a gentle squeeze. "I want to help. I promise. But I can't do that unless we get you into the apartment." She thought for a second. "Unless you have a wheelchair, or maybe a walker in there somewhere."

"No. No wheelchair. Let's just do it."

She helped him swing his legs around until they were both on the ground. "Okay, whenever you're ready. Grab my wrists."

She moved her hands lower until they wrapped around his forearm and waited for him to do the same. "It'll be stronger this way. I'll be less likely to drop you." She said the words with a smile only to hear him swear again. A little louder this time.

"On the count of three. *Um...dois...tres!*"

That did it. He was out of the car, although he was holding most of his weight on his right leg.

It was no better evidently.

"Okay, we're going to do like we did before. Lean your weight on me." She sensed an argument forming and cut him off. "We can work on the cane once we get into the house."

They made their way to the elevator, and she let him push the button. Sixth floor. "How many floors is this building?"

"Six."

Okay, so he was on the top floor. Once the elevator reached number six, and the doors opened, she realized there were only two doors up here. So these apartments had to be huge. The floor she lived on had six residences on it. "Are your keys on the same ring as your car keys?"

"Yes." The words came out in a short burst of air that told her his strength was flagging.

She quickly fished them out of her pocket and held one of the keys up. He nodded and reached for it, opening the door so fast that she almost lost her balance. She caught herself just in time. It would have been great to say *trust me* and then have them both collapse into the apartment.

She got him as far as the couch and lowered him onto it before saying, "Wait here. I'll be right back."

CHAPTER EIGHT

ROQUE HAD TENSED when she'd joked about him having a wheelchair in his apartment. He didn't. Not anymore. What he did still have was a walker. It was hidden inside a closet in his spare bedroom. He could barely look at his old nemesis without myriad emotions clutching at his gut and threatening to rob the strength from his legs.

He'd gone from a young man who could dance his way through a clump of football players on his way to making one goal after another, to a man who could barely put one foot in front of the other—even with the help of that walker. A man who'd aged twenty years overnight.

He'd always meant to donate it, but he didn't like looking at it, much less try to drag it down to his car.

His body had failed him once, and it looked like it was failing him again.

As much as he tried to suppress it, a hole of fear opened up inside him. What if, despite what he'd said, it wasn't just his muscle? What if the fall onto his ass had knocked something loose, or torn a muscle that he couldn't afford to lose?

His cat appeared from the kitchen and came over and hopped into his lap. He picked her up and set her beside him. "Sorry, girl. I'll feed you as soon as I can get back up."

Amy reappeared with a trash can and he tensed. "I'm not going to vomit, if that's what you're worried about."

"Of course not. I took the liner out of it and it's clean. I'm going to put some hot towels in there, but I need to know where your dryer is because I'm going to rotate moist heat with dry." She stopped. "Aw…is that Rachel?"

"Yes."

Amy came over and tickled the cat's head, trailing her fingers over Rachel's thick fur. "Hi, there. I've heard about you. Lucky girl,

I don't have allergies." Her head suddenly came up and she glanced away from him. "Dryer?"

"I don't have a dryer, but I do have a heating pad."

"Where?"

He nodded toward his bedroom door. "In the closet in my spare bedroom on the top shelf."

Moving toward where he'd indicated, she slid through the bedroom door, reappearing two minutes later. "Okay, so you do have something."

When he looked up, he saw she was holding the heating pad in one hand, and the walker in the other.

"No. Put that away. Right now."

His voice was forceful enough that Rachel hopped off the couch, giving him a baleful glance as she stalked away. But the last thing he wanted to see was a reminder of how weak he'd once been. How utterly helpless he'd felt. Especially when faced with a woman who'd had to help him walk to his own damned car.

Amy set the walker down with a frown.

"It's not for forever, it's just to give your leg muscles a break tonight."

"Not tonight. Not ever."

She stared him down for several minutes before leaving the walker where it was and coming over with the heating pad. "Okay, we'll talk about it later."

No, they wouldn't. But damn, she was as stubborn as he was. An unwilling smile came to the surface, despite his best efforts to keep it down. "I wouldn't count on that."

All she did was laugh—a knowing little laugh that said she was going to get her way. Some way or another. Maybe she normally did, since she was the power person in her little physical therapy realm. But she was in his world now. And here, he was used to calling the shots.

Only he was pretty sure that Amy wasn't easily intimidated.

"Let me get set up. It'll just take a few minutes, but in the meantime, I'll plug this in and get some heat going to those muscles. Take off your pants."

Shock rolled through him. There was no

way in hell. That was almost as bad as her suggestion to use a walker.

"Not happening. You can do whatever it is you want to do through them."

"No. I can't. Not only can't I, but I won't. I have a towel here." She pulled something out of her beach bag. A huge pink towel with a picture of cats.

"What is that?"

"It's an *Aristocats* towel. You know—like the movie? You can drape it over your lap, since you seem to be so, er, modest." She said it with a twitch of her lips.

Modest. Sure. He could show her exactly how modest he was. Because despite the pain in his leg and the pain she was in his backside right now, there was a very real possibility that at some point that towel might reveal a muscle problem of an entirely different kind.

"I'll help you take them off, then." Her smile was teasing. Coaxing. And something shifted inside of him. Something he didn't want to examine. And he certainly didn't want her to catch a glimpse of it in his expression. He had to get rid of her for a minute or two, even if it meant taking his damn pants off.

"Fine. Go in the other room, and I'll get them off myself." He would do it if it killed him.

"Okey dokey." She tossed the cat towel in his lap and picked up the trash can and stack of towels and carried it into the kitchen. "Yell when you're ready. Or when you decide you need some help."

He'd just unbuttoned his jeans when she popped her head back into the room. Was she kidding him? "What?"

"I think Rachel is hungry. What does she eat?"

"There are cans in the pantry and her dish is on the floor beside the dishwasher."

This time she stayed gone, while he did his best to shimmy out of the snug garment, sweat beading his lip when he had to put too much weight on his injured leg.

Diabos. What if he had to have surgery on it? Again. Worse, what if he could no longer *perform* surgeries? Or perform at all.

After his accident, it had been two years before he'd gotten the nerve up to actually try to have sex with someone. Some of that was because of Halee's betrayal, but some of it was also due to his *body's* betrayal.

Well, there was certainly no sign of that kind of trouble tonight. In fact...

He yanked his right foot out of the leg of the jeans and used it to push them off his other leg. He picked up the towel that sported a white cat with a big pink bow around her neck and a smaller one on top of her head.

Caramba! He draped the ridiculous thing over his legs, wondering why he hadn't asked her to leave one of his plain white towels instead. Because they weren't as big as this one was, of course.

A few minutes later, she came back in with the trash can. Curls of steam came out of the top of it.

He frowned. "Exactly how hot are those towels?"

"Pretty hot."

He glanced at her. Several strands of hair had escaped her ponytail, spiraling down her collarbone. And with her standing there in a white sundress that sported tiny little holes all over it, Roque was struck with the thought that the towels weren't the only thing in this room that were hot. Amy was, too. Even the pain in his leg couldn't erase what she did to him. And then there were her feet.

Bare feet.

"What happened to your shoes?"

"They're in my beach bag."

Thinking back, he didn't think she'd put them back on as she helped him walk back to the car. The pavement had to be blistering hot, but she'd said nothing. And she'd driven his car barefooted. Had come up in the elevator like that and padded across his wood floors.

And that was the impetus he needed to do what she asked. If she could do what was necessary for him, he was going to cooperate with whatever she wanted him to do.

That immediately sent another flurry of thoughts spinning through his head that had no business being there.

"Will the moisture hurt your couch? If so, we'll move this operation to your floor. Or…your bed."

Um…no. Not the bed.

"It won't hurt the couch. And the back folds down to make a bed." The black leather was pretty forgiving.

"That's perfect. How does it work?"

"There's a button on the side of it." He leaned forward so the back wouldn't go sailing down with him on it.

She cranked it down. "Okay. Is the pain in front or in back?"

Even as she said it, a little twinge happened that he needed to suppress—that had to do with a pain of another kind. "It's actually on the outside of my thigh, where the scar is."

"Let's have you lie on your stomach, then, like we would if this were a massage table."

His stomach. Good choice. He relaxed slightly. "I want the towel wrapped around my waist, then."

"Your wish is my command."

And that was a phrase he didn't even want to consider. Because what he suddenly wished for, he couldn't have. Like kisses. The kind they'd shared in his office.

Between the two of them, they somehow

got him covered and in position. Then there was a quick sting as she draped one of the hot towels over his left leg and then another on top of that. Then she set the timer on her phone and pulled a vial out of her purse.

He gave it a wary look. Had she gotten some kind of herbal potion from Flávia Maura? "What is that?"

"Relax. It's just a blend of essential oils that I carry around for muscle pain. It has wintergreen, peppermint, lemongrass and a few other things in it. I'm going to mix it with some olive oil I found in your pantry. It will act as a natural analgesic and will help lubricate the skin as I work it." She paused. "Unless you want to take a muscle relaxer. If you have some."

He did somewhere, but he tried to avoid taking them, having had a problem weaning himself off narcotic painkillers after the accident. It had made him leery of taking much of anything. "I'd rather not unless I have to."

"That's what I thought."

She took the towels off and traded them

for another two. "Once these cool, I'm going to massage your muscles, using the oils."

Massage his muscles. Great. Well, there was one muscle that he was glad she couldn't see.

Five minutes later her hands were on him. And as soon as her touch hit his skin the pain in his leg became so much background noise. It was there, but it was not what his primary focus was. Her hands squeezed and rubbed and worked in strong capable strokes that had his eyes closing. Only to jerk back apart when she got to the seized area.

"Diabos!"

"Hurt?"

"Yes."

"Good."

His head cranked around to look at her only to have her smile. "I can feel the balled-up muscles, but needed you to tell me I was in the right spot."

"Oh, you're in the right spot, all right."

He gritted his teeth and willed the pain away, forgetting about almost everything else. But still she kept working, kneading, using the base of her palm to push against the tightness in his leg. Fifteen minutes later he realized the pain was ebbing, so slowly he wasn't aware of when it had actually started retreating, but it was fifty percent better. Then sixty. Then seventy-five. And that he could live with.

"Thank you. I think it worked."

"Just give me a few minutes longer. I think I can get the rest of it."

True to her word, when her hands finally went still, her fingers paused to trace the furrow of his scar, sending a shudder through him. She'd taken almost every bit of his pain away. And added a pain from a completely different source.

"Amy, thank you."

Her hand moved away, and he immediately wanted it back.

"You're welcome."

He cautiously rolled over and sat up, keeping the towel in place, and felt no flare in his leg. When he looked at her, though, her cheeks were flushed in a way that might have been exertion, but it also might be...

She'd traced his scar, her fingers soft and sure, and had felt totally different from what she had done moments earlier. It had hit him on an emotional level that was new to him. He normally did not like women lingering over that mark.

She was still kneeling on the rug in front of the sofa, but when she went to grab one of the towels on the floor, he stopped her with a hand to her wrist. Then, unable to resist, he stroked a finger along her cheek. "Leave all of the stuff, and I'll get it in the morning."

"How are you feeling?" She peered up at him with eyes that almost sparkled. And he found he liked it. Wanted to be the reason for that look.

"Better. I can't believe a simple massage had that much of an effect."

In reality, there'd been nothing simple about that massage. Or the effect it had had on him.

"I told you it would work. Do you believe me now?"

"I believe…*you*. I once had another physical therapist, though, who…" Not finishing his sentence, he stood, hauling her to her feet, her hands warming his and sending an answering heat straight to the area he'd been trying to ignore. He stared down at her face, watching as her teeth found her lower lip and pressed deep into the soft skin.

Damn. He should have stayed down on the couch, because now that he was standing, all he wanted to do was...

Kiss her.

He cupped her face, and she tilted it as if waiting. For him. "Hell, Amy. What was in those oils again?"

"Nothing dangerous."

That's where she was wrong. Because something powerful was coursing through his veins, taking control of his thoughts. And if he was reading her expression correctly, she was feeling its effects, too.

"Hey." His thumbs stroked along her jawline, the soft skin creating an addiction that he didn't want to fight. "If I kissed you—in this ridiculous towel—what would you do?"

A dimple played peekaboo in her cheek. "Maybe you should try it and find out."

Her smile said this was one time that she

wasn't going to put him on the ground with a sweep of her leg.

So Roque lowered his head and slid his mouth against hers.

The second he touched her lips, Amy melted inside. She'd enjoyed the last fifteen minutes of that massage far too much. His muscles were firm beneath his skin, not flaccid the way she would expect them to be. He felt like an athlete. Even though he was no longer one.

His lips were firm as well, moving over hers in a way that sparked tiny fires of need all along her nerve endings. God, she couldn't believe this was happening. It was like he'd somehow read her thoughts and was thanking her for making him feel better.

Only this didn't feel like it was done out of duty. Or gratitude. It felt like he wanted her as much as she wanted him.

A fling. Wasn't that what she'd envisioned having with some stranger? Hadn't she seen it as a way to jump-start her life and send her in a new direction?

Well, who needed a stranger when she

had the perfect man right here in her arms. Someone she knew…trusted. Someone who was safe. Someone whose skin she'd already touched and wanted to touch again. In a completely different way.

She didn't need commitment. Didn't want it. Not the way she'd wanted it in the past, only to be disappointed when the man she'd cared about had suddenly pulled away without so much as an excuse or a goodbye. That had hurt. Enough to not want to repeat that experience.

But she didn't need promises of a future from this particular man.

Amy settled in to enjoy, wanting nothing more than to be swept to bed and revel in his lovemaking.

Only he wasn't going to be able to sweep her up in his arms. And that was okay. She didn't need shows of strength. She just needed him, and what he could do for her.

Her hands slid up his arms, loving the way his muscles corded beneath her touch, her fingers continuing their upward journey, before tunneling into the warm hair just above the collar of his polo shirt.

Roque's head tilted, deepening the kiss, his palms skimming down the back of her dress, before pulling away slightly. He fingered the fabric. "What's the name of this?" he asked as he bunched the skirt in his hands, the cool air in his apartment caressing the backs of her thighs in a way that made her squirm against him. "I haven't been able to stop thinking about it all day."

"About what?" Her mind glazed over, having a hard time thinking beyond what she felt at the front of his towel.

He smiled against her mouth. "This material with its tiny little holes. It looks so sweet and innocent, but there's a warm sexy side to it that makes me want to explore each and every inch of it."

Thank God that bubbling awareness hadn't been completely one-sided. She'd been more and more conscious of it as the day went by. At least until she'd kicked his feet out from under him.

"Eyelet. I don't know what it is in Portuguese."

"Mmm… I don't, either." His lips ran over her jawline and down her throat, the heat from his mouth almost unbearable. And when he reached the sweetheart neckline of the dress, he brushed along the dips and curves, making her moan. Still keeping the fabric behind her gathered up, he used the fingers of his other hand to find the zipper at the back of her dress, easing it down until he reached her waist. Then he traveled back up, finding the strap of her bra and tugging it slightly. "So you do have one on. This time."

So he had noticed that first day that she wasn't wearing one. Her senses went up in flames.

She didn't want him laying her down on the couch, since she'd worked on him there. This was one time when she really didn't want to mix business with pleasure. Plus, Rachel had come out a couple of times, trying to get their attention, and Amy would rather not have to share Roque with her right now.

Maybe he read her thoughts, because he gave her mouth a hard kiss. "I'm thinking I'd like to be somewhere else. Somewhere a little more private."

Relief swamped through her.

"I was just thinking that myself," she murmured.

Letting her dress go, he took her hand and pulled her along with him until he reached the back of the apartment, going through a door, which he nudged shut behind them. She took a second to take in her surroundings.

A huge bed, clad in a plain brown quilted spread, sat in the center of the room, large wooden posts making it both masculine and inviting at the same time.

Or maybe that was Roque.

Reaching the bottom of her dress, he hauled it up and over her head, until she stood there wearing only her underwear and her bra, both pink. He fingered the waistline of the lacy briefs. "Are these…?"

She tilted her head. "Are they what?"

"The same underwear that were hanging out of your suitcase that first day?"

Her face flamed to life, remembering the circumstances of that visit. "Yes, they were." Had she subconsciously worn them today, thinking this was where they were going to wind up?

No, there's no way she could have planned any of this.

"They've haunted me for weeks."

She laughed. "And here I was hoping you hadn't noticed them."

He reached down as if he were going to scoop her up in his arms, but she stopped him by stepping out of reach.

"What's wrong?"

A lot of conflicting emotions chased across his face, making her realize he'd misunderstood why she'd moved away. "I don't want you lifting me. Or doing anything that might make that leg act up again. That would make me very unhappy, in more ways than one." She glanced at the bed and then went over and pulled the spread down to the halfway point. "Why don't you lie down?"

"I am not some invalid, Amy."

"Oh, believe me, I know that." To hide the quick ache in her heart his words had caused, she forced a laugh and reached for his towel, whisking it away. He stood there in boxer briefs that gave very clear evidence of what he was feeling. "There. That's more like it."

"You are impossible." But he said it with a smile that chased the ache away. "But there's something else I need. In the nightstand."

Going over to it, she opened the top drawer and found a package of condoms. He was right. They did need something. She'd almost forgotten about protection. Tossing them on the bed, she grinned at him.

"Anything else?"

He nodded. "Yes. If I promise not to do any kind of gymnastics, will you let me take an active role?"

"How active?" She needed to tread carefully.

Coming over to stand in front of her, he gripped her hips and hauled her against him. "Enough to get the job done. For both of us." His gaze turned serious. "Don't put me back in that walker, even in my head. I've been there, and I didn't much like it."

She hadn't been trying to do that, but could see how he might feel a little insecure right now, since she'd been in a place of power as she'd worked on him. Something in her wanted to press the point, but an inner voice warned her that this was one battle she didn't want to win. Because in winning, she would lose.

"An invalid is not what I think of when I look at you. But no gymnastics."

"Not this time."

He didn't try to pick her up again; instead, keeping his hands on her hips, he walked her backward until the backs of her thighs hit the mattress. Then he gave her a soft push and down she went, bouncing a time or two on the soft surface. It felt luxurious and heady, and exactly what she'd been thinking of when she'd imagined being with someone.

The bed was high enough that she could picture him doing all kinds of things to her, and that was enough to make her squirm.

Maybe he sensed it, because he stood over her for a minute and then reached for the pink lace at her hips and peeled it down her thighs. She straightened her legs so he wouldn't have to bend getting them down her calves and then they were off.

"Meu Deus. Você é a mulher mais linda do mundo."

She wasn't the most beautiful woman in

the world, but it was nice to hear him say the words. And to hear that her dress had turned him on. And right now she couldn't imagine being any more turned on than she was at this moment.

When he acted like he was going to bend over to kiss her, though, she planted her bare foot on his stomach. "Stay as straight as you can."

"Bossy. So very bossy. But okay. I'll stay all the way up here and just do…this."

He used a leg to part her knees, then wrapped his hands around her thighs and dragged her to the edge of the bed. Then he was right there. Up close and personal.

"Better?" he asked.

"Yes." Her body was on fire.

"But first—" he motioned to an area beside her arm "—I'm going to need that packet."

Oh! That's right. She opened the cardboard box and retrieved one, ripping it open and tossing it to him. He caught it with ease, and set it over her navel. Then he reached down and pulled his shirt over his head and stepped out of his briefs, while Amy unhooked her bra and flung it toward the end of the bed, where it ended up getting caught on one of the bedposts.

He sheathed himself. "Sit up, *querida*."

She did what he asked and realized almost immediately why when he cupped her breasts, stroking the nipples between his fingers and squeezing.

"Ah…" Her arms went behind her to support herself, arching her back and pushing herself into his touch.

"What you do to me…"

His voice had roughened, tones lowering until they were deep-edged with need. Or at least she hoped it was.

Then he reached to cup her bottom and entered her with a quick thrust that stretched her…filled her. Her eyes might have rolled back in her head—she wasn't quite sure. All she knew was that this was like no encounter she'd ever had before. There was normally a lot of foreplay and give and take, but Roque wasn't interested in her doing anything evidently.

She'd been ready to sit and ride him to completion to save his leg from any pain.

But what she saw on his face wasn't pain. It was need. Lust. A bunch of things mixed up together that she didn't understand.

What she did know was that she wanted him. Wanted this. Didn't want it to stop.

Except it would, because she was slipping closer and closer to the edge of a cliff, and once off, there would be no going back.

She didn't care, though. Only knew that as he continued to push into her body and then retreat that she was about as close to heaven as she was ever likely to get.

Tipping her face up, he kissed her as he continued to move, wrapping both arms around her back, using his tongue in ways that put every one of her nerve endings on high alert.

"I've wanted this. Almost since you arrived."

That made two of them. "Me too."

She wanted to say more, but the words wouldn't form, wouldn't come, and she was afraid if she said them she might mutter something that she couldn't take back, so she clamped her teeth together. Then she felt him there, seeking entrance, and she pried them back apart. The second his tongue entered her mouth, it was almost too much, and her hands went to the back of his head to hold him there, even as her legs circled his back and pulled him in closer.

"Amy... I'm not going to be able to..."

One of his hands slid between their bodies, seeking something. Finding it. Squeezing and sliding his thumb over that sensitized nub of flesh.

"Go, Roque. Oh, go!" The words came out in a frantic rush that he must have recognized, because he thrust into her at a speed that drove the air from her lungs, even as the edge of that cliff rushed forward and collided with her, sending her over the edge in an instant. Her body spasmed around him as he continued to surge inside of her, giving gritted mutterings that slid past her ear and escaped into the air around them.

Still he thrust into her, taking a minute or two before he slowed, letting her sink back to the bed, where she lay nerveless and still.

He reached under her and held her tight against him as if knowing what was coming. "No. Not yet."

She echoed those words in her head, knowing once that happened, once they came apart, she was going to be left to try to pick up the shattered pieces of her composure. And she was going to be faced with the reality of what they'd done.

She'd gotten her fling.

But she was very afraid she might have gotten something more than she bargained for—something that wouldn't be easy to put behind her.

All she knew was that she was going to have to try.

But today, he was headed down to the
physical therapy department, where Amy
was having her first session with Enzo. He
intended to be there when it ended and pick
his up. Even though he wasn't entirely sure
what that meant.

All he knew was that he hadn't liked the
way things had ended in his apartment.

CHAPTER NINE

THERE WAS AN elephant in the room that
someone didn't want to talk about. And it
wasn't him. Worse, his mom told him that
she'd sent Amy a card inviting her to a
party she was having, but that she hadn't
yet RSVP'd. She wanted Roque to "ask" her
to come—meaning, coax her into coming.

He was going to do nothing of the sort,
although the phone call prompted him to
do what he'd been putting off for the last
two weeks, as he'd watched Amy frantically
work alongside of the other members of the
team and then drop just as quickly off the
radar. As if she was avoiding being alone
with him.

As if?

No, there was no question about what she
was doing.

But today, he was headed down to the physical therapy department, where Amy was having her first session with Enzo. He intended to be there when it ended and have his say. Even though he wasn't entirely sure what that was.

All he knew was that he hadn't liked the way things had ended in his apartment. She'd slid out the door almost before he'd caught his breath.

The elevator doors opened and a large open room stood in front of him.

It was a beehive of activity with patients posted in different stations working on whatever task their therapist had given them.

There. He spotted Enzo.

The man gave him a quick wave. He'd passed his swallow test a couple of weeks ago with flying colors, but Roque didn't expect anything different from his old coach. He walked toward Enzo, noticing that while Amy was also there, she didn't quite meet his eyes when she looked at him.

Addressing Enzo, he asked, "How's it going?"

"She hasn't made me cry yet."

His words came out a little garbled because of the changes they'd made to his jaw, but at least he could talk. He was doing speech therapy as well and they were all hopeful that there was no nerve damage. Krysta didn't think there was. She'd been meticulous in her resection of everything. That muscle memory was just going to have to kick back in at some point.

And he was sure it would. It was just a matter of practice and reopening those neural pathways.

"Don't worry, she's still got a month and a half to work on you—there's still plenty of time."

However, Roque had decided he couldn't put off his discussion with Amy any longer.

They'd done nothing morally wrong, but her attitude told him that *she* believed they'd made a mistake. And on some level, so did he. He just couldn't put his finger on why.

This was a temporary assignment for her. And, actually, for him as well. So logically that should make it easier to resolve. But so far, it hadn't.

She really had helped his leg. The day

after she'd worked on it he'd only felt a tiny twinge of discomfort that had worked itself out as the day went on. So when he'd told her physical therapy could no longer help him, he'd been wrong. It had been a knee-jerk reaction to what had happened long before she came on the scene.

"I'm feeling better," Enzo managed to get out.

Roque put his hand on his friend's shoulder. "I'm so glad. It must feel good to be at the last part of your journey." He remembered when he was almost done with medical school. The elation and fear he'd felt as he faced the future ahead of him.

Enzo was probably feeling some of that as well.

"He's worked hard today. Hard enough that I'm ready to let him off the hook. At least until next week." Amy smiled, but it was aimed at Enzo rather than him. "Make sure you do those exercises I gave you. They'll really help get your range of motion back again."

Enzo nodded and hopped off the table. They said their goodbyes, and Roque's friend headed for the double doors that connected the physical therapy area with the rest of the hospital.

Once he was gone, Roque turned back to face her. "Do you have another patient right now?"

"No, that was my last one for the day."

"Good. Do you think we can find someplace to talk?"

Her eyes closed for a second before opening. "About what?"

A muscle tightened in his jaw. "I think you know what this is about."

"Yes, I think I do." She sighed and this time looked at him. "Let's take a walk."

She started, then stopped. "How's your leg?"

"It's fine. And yes, before you ask, I am more than capable of walking."

"I didn't mean that."

He wasn't sure why he'd snapped at her. Maybe it was just that he missed some of that quick back-and-forth *jogo de palavras* they'd had before. There was no hint of that teasing manner now. Everything was stilted and formal. Professional. Just like he'd wanted. Right?

"I'm sorry. Let's go to the *pátio*."

Behind the hospital there was a small private garden area with benches where patients or relatives could get out and enjoy the sun or sit under the shade of one of the trees. It reminded him a little of his parents' *chácara* with its greenery. It was also fairly private, with little chance of anyone overhearing them.

They got out to the courtyard and slowly made their way down the bricked path. "I don't actually think I've been out here yet. It's beautiful."

"It is. I came out here a lot when I was a medical student."

She glanced at him. "I didn't realize you did your studies at Paulista."

"I did. I felt like I needed a change of scenery from Rio."

"Your parents moved here to be near you?"

"My mom's family is from São Paulo, so she had no problem relocating. To a Brazilian—as you probably know—family is everything."

He wasn't quite sure how the conversation had turned in this direction, but it beat the chilly silence he'd tried to ignore for the last couple of weeks. And she'd seemed to relax into the conversation.

"I was always surprised my mom didn't move back to Brazil after my dad died."

"To be near your uncle, you mean?"

Maybe if he brought her thoughts back to her reasons for coming to Brazil, they could both move past the awkwardness of what had happened.

"Yes. She said she and my uncle hadn't spoken in years, though. He disagreed with her marrying so young and so quickly and moving to the States."

Amy hadn't told her uncle about her mother's death. It wasn't the kind of news she'd wanted to break to him over the phone, especially when the man was traveling on business.

Roque wanted to keep her talking, not only because it might help them regain their footing, but also because he genuinely wanted to know. She'd come here because of her mom, to learn a little more about her roots, so maybe he could help her flesh some of that out.

"Did your mom grow up where your uncle lives now?"

"I don't know. She didn't talk much about her life in Brazil. As far as I know, she only came back to Brazil once to visit. When I was a baby. My uncle evidently refused to see her."

"I bet he regrets that now."

"I think maybe he does. At least he didn't refuse to see me." She sighed. "I think the problem was that my mom didn't give him time to process what was happening between her and my dad. My dad worked for one of the major car manufacturers, which has a plant here in São Paulo. He and my mom met on one of his business trips and fell in love. Three weeks later, they were married and heading to Florida. I was born a year after that."

"That was quick."

Amy smiled. "That was my mom. She lived in the moment and gave herself fully to it, not looking back. Maybe that's part of the reason why once she left Brazil, she was loath to come back."

That thought skated through his head for a minute. So once Amy left Brazil would she do the same and never come back?

That sent a pang through him. But it also might mean that if Amy lived in the moment, she would be able to put what had happened between them in the past and not look back at it.

"Do you think you'll come back to visit?"

"I think that depends on how things with my uncle go."

Roque's leg was starting to get tired, so he found a bench and motioned her to it. Sliding onto the seat, he stretched his leg out in front of him to ease the ache.

"So it is bothering you—I thought so."

"Not much. It just gets tired."

"There are some machines back at the—"

He tensed. "I don't want to talk about the machines. I want to talk about what happened back at the apartment."

Her chin went up and she looked him in the eye. "What about it?"

Well, he could name a whole lot of things, but since he'd brought it up, he needed to get to the crux of the issue and confront it. "Things have been awkward. And I'd like to get past that, if we can."

"I don't know if I can, Roque."

The enormity of those words was a punch to the gut. But before he could formulate a response, she went on. "I've never had sex… well, outside of a dating relationship, and certainly never with a patient. It was unprofessional and I—"

So that's what this was about.

"Let's get one thing straight. I am not your patient."

Her shoulders sagged. "I thought maybe you would wonder if I got involved with—" her hand made a little flourish in the air "—I don't know, people like Enzo or other patients."

Roque turned to look her in the eye. "After my injury, I had a physical therapist in Rio who wanted more from me. She tried to draw out my treatment even after I stopped making progress. Believe me, if I even sensed you were like that, you would be out of the program in a heartbeat." He nudged her shoulder. "You didn't take advantage of me. I wanted what happened as much as you did. We were two people who came together for one night, just like so many others before us."

She smiled. "You have no idea how much better that makes me feel. Well, since we're sharing confidences, I had toyed with the possibility of having a fling with a handsome Brazilian."

"A fling?" His brows went up. "You mean like a *caso*?"

"I don't know what that word means. Like an affair?"

He nodded. "Except neither of us is—" he tried to think of the word "—linked with someone."

"No, we're not. So you're right. I think maybe I made too much of it. Like I said, I was worried about how you might view what we did."

"I view it as completely unimportant."

Something shifted in her eyes, a quick flicker of hurt that made him pause. He'd expected relief, not this…uncertainty. He'd sensed a lack of confidence in her once or twice before. Only this time it wasn't related to her work. It was related to him. "Is that not the right word?"

Her arms wrapped around her waist. "It's exactly the right word."

Except she was no longer looking at him. "Maybe 'inconsequential' would have been a better choice?"

Nothing changed in her face. "Those are both good words to describe it."

An uneasiness gathered in his chest. He wasn't sure where it came from or why her reaction mattered. It shouldn't. He was happy with his life the way it was. No entanglements. No commitments. No one to worry about where he might wind up ten years down the road.

Seeing her holding that walker in his living room had sent acid swirling in his gut. It was like a foreshadowing of what his future might hold. Maybe it was even the reason he'd never brought himself to get rid of the thing.

He did not want to be treated like an invalid. Not by Amy. Not by anyone. It had been ridiculous to feel that way with her. And yet he had—had suddenly felt like he had something to prove, despite her words to the contrary. There was no changing it.

He pushed forward toward his original goal in bringing her out here. "So things between us are good?"

"Yes, Roque, they're good. We should just put it behind us."

And yet the stiltedness was back in her speech. He'd said something wrong, and he had no idea what it was. But he really did want to try to undo it.

So he said something crazy. So crazy he had no idea where the words had come from. "My mom told me she invited you to her party. She very much would like for you to come. And so would I."

Dammit. What the hell are you doing?

"I don't know…"

"It's nothing formal, so there'd no chance that I could step on your dress this time."

She smiled. Finally, and her expression transformed in an instant. "I stepped on it a couple of times myself that night, if you remember. I was very glad my tae kwon do instructor wasn't there to see me."

Mentioning the invitation was the right thing to do. He wasn't sure how or why, but it had clicked something in that beautiful face of hers. "I think he would have been pretty proud of the way you took me down at the beach."

She laughed. "I finally got to see how it works outside of a classroom setting."

"It was quite effective." He paused, then went back to his question. "So you'll come to the house?"

"If you're sure they don't mind. I thought maybe your mom was just being polite."

"Believe me, she wouldn't have invited you if she didn't want you there."

"When is it again?" She got to her feet.

"On the eighteenth."

"I think it depends on whether the head of the department wants me to work or not. He's a pretty intimidating guy."

He got to his feet as well, and it took him a second to realize she was talking about him. He laughed. "Not so intimidating. And no. I'm giving us that night off."

"Okay, it sounds great. Thank you."

Things might not be exactly back to where they were before this had happened. But at least they were on cordial footing again. Hopefully he could keep it that way. At least for the rest of her stay.

Amy picked up a dress off the rack, before putting it back with a sigh. She needed to hurry. Her uncle was finally back from his trip and she was planning on taking a cab to his house as soon as she finished here.

Maybe she should skip shopping and just wear the eyelet sundress she'd worn to the beach again.

No. That dress was going to be permanently retired. She couldn't look at it without remembering Roque's long fingers worrying one of the holes and trying to figure out what kind of fabric it was.

Although their work relationship was better now, there were still flashes from that conversation in the garden that came back to bite her.

Her stomach twisted.

Roque viewed their night together as "unimportant." And it was. He'd been technically right. But still, to hear those words coming from this particular man's mouth had sent shock crashing through her. Changing the term to *inconsequential* had just made it worse.

That's the damn definition of a fling, Amy. Isn't that what you said you wanted? It was one night. Not six months.

She shuffled through more dresses, getting more and more irritated with herself.

Why did you even agree to go to his parents' party?

Because of something she'd seen in his face. Something that said it wasn't as unimportant as he'd said.

And she liked his parents. She really hadn't had a chance to talk with many people outside of the hospital program. This was a chance to get to know life, as her mom had once known it. At least that was what she told herself. And, in reality, she hadn't seen Roque as much in the last week or two as she had in the first half of the program while shadowing him. And she missed it. Missed being invited to watch surgeries, being asked about her opinion on cases. She even missed seeing Peter and Lara, who were still in the orthopedics department.

Roque still technically oversaw her, but as the program was set up to do, she had been passed over to the physical therapy side of things. Enzo's PT sessions were going amazingly well, and periodically Roque had come down to watch. She now found herself watching to see if he would come through that door, which she hated, but it was like her eyes were instilled with a homing device that kept trying to track him down.

At the end of the month, they would all say their goodbyes at the sendoff party, and she would get on a plane and fly back home.

Home?

For the first time in her life Florida didn't quite feel like home anymore. But her life was there. Her career. Her future doctorate work would be done there. She couldn't just uproot herself and come live in Brazil. She barely knew anyone except for Roque, Krysta and Flávia and a few other people at the hospital. And most of those would be leaving when the summer program was over.

Amy shook off those thoughts and picked up another casual dress, although Roque said jeans would be fine. Most Brazilians loved their denim and wore it for a lot of different occasions.

Actually, maybe she would wear jeans. She had a pair that were dark and slim-fitting and showed off her figure. She hoped, anyway.

Why?

Maybe she really did have something to prove. To herself, if nothing else. She'd had her fling—she kept using that term, although could one night technically be considered a fling? She had no idea, since she'd never had one before. But there was still something in her that wasn't satisfied—that wanted more.

But never mind that. She needed to decide on an outfit, and quickly. She was supposed to be at her uncle's house in an hour. It looked like jeans it was. So giving the salesperson an apologetic smile, she headed out the door, looking for the nearest taxi stand.

CHAPTER TEN

THE DAY OF the party arrived and Amy found she was almost as nervous getting ready for this event as she'd been over the cookout at the *chácara*. So much had happened between then and now. She'd visited a beach with Roque, had had sex with him at his apartment. And had visited an uncle she'd never met.

She and Abel had laughed and cried over memories of her mom, and he'd expressed a lifetime of regret over having turned her away all those years ago when she came to visit. He'd promised he and his wife would come visit her in the States once she got back.

The calendar seemed to suddenly be tripping over itself, the dates cascading past like a waterfall. But she wasn't going to think about that. Not tonight.

She tugged on her slim-fitting dark-washed jeans, pulling out a pair of heeled boots to go with them. She then dropped a slinky green top over her head, cinching it at the waist with the same silver-linked belt she'd worn for the welcome party. That soiree seemed like a lifetime ago.

Pulling her hair back in a sleek ponytail and brushing on a coat of mascara and some gloss on her lips, she declared herself ready.

Roque had offered to come get her, but she'd opted to take a taxi instead. Maybe for the same reason she'd packed away that eyelet dress.

Forty-five minutes later, she arrived, walking up the driveway to the sound of laughter. She suddenly wondered just how big of a party this was, and the urge to turn around and run after her taxi welled up inside of her before she shoved it away.

She'd told them she would be here, and there would be questions if she didn't show. Ringing the buzzer at the gate, she leaned down expecting a voice to come over the intercom system. Instead, the door opened and Roque's mom flew down the walkway, clicking open the gate. She gave Amy a kiss on the cheek, which by now she was accustomed to.

"É bom vê-lo novamente!"

The enthusiasm in the woman's voice erased any doubts she might have had about coming. *"Obrigada pelo convite."*

Roque had been right on that front. Exchanging pleasantries in Portuguese had become a lot easier as the weeks marched by. Her tongue no longer tripped over half of the words. She still spoke to Roque in English, however. Somehow it seemed more important to get the words right when addressing him. She still hadn't quite figured out why. Only that it mattered in a way she didn't understand.

If he minded her speaking in English, he didn't let on. He just kept responding in kind, while tossing in a smattering of Portuguese words when he was unsure of something.

Like "unimportant"?

"Come in, come in. Andre is hoping to be

home before dinner. He had an emergency call come in a few minutes ago."

With all these people here, it looked like it was sink or swim as far as Portuguese went.

But it was only dinner. She could last an hour or two before her mind went numb from trying to find words.

She followed Claudia into the house and found a charming array of blue and white tile and clean textiles. It was completely different from their *chácara*, but not in a bad way. The space was spotless, and the scents... Her mouth watered.

"Is there anything I can help with?"

"You can keep my son from causing trouble." Claudia said it with a mischievous smile that made her stomach flip.

What kind of trouble?

She didn't know, but as if summoned the man was suddenly walking toward her in black jeans and a white shirt, his sleeves rolled up to reveal tanned arms. Arms that she had seen and felt and...

Ack! No. No thinking about what she had seen of the man. She was pretty sure his mom would not approve of the images racing through her head.

His cane was nowhere to be seen. Wait. No, there it was. By the front door. He evidently was feeling okay.

"You came." He smiled, taking one of her hands and squeezing it.

A warm buzz of electricity traveled up her arm and burst into pinpoints of heat throughout her body. Yep. It was still there. That awareness that had been there since the very first moment when he'd stepped on her dress. She'd learned so much about him since that time. Had seen a few of his insecurities and had witnessed his incredible, resilient strength.

"I told you I would."

"I know, but when you said you'd take a taxi I had doubts. I am glad you're here."

She didn't tell him she'd very nearly crawled back in that taxi and left. The sincerity in his voice made her glad she'd stayed. As did the fingers that were still gripping hers.

He wanted her here. Unlike when she'd

first applied to come, when he admitted he'd very nearly said no.

So much had changed since their first meeting all those weeks ago.

The pinpricks grew in size, attacking her belly…her chest…

Her heart.

She swallowed.

Oh, don't, Amy. Don't. Do not!

It was too late. All the mental lectures in the world were not going to change anything. She was in love with the man.

A giggle came out before she could stop it as a realization struck her. She was a little more like her mom than she thought. But what had taken Cecília Rodrigo Woodell little more than a moment to admit—that she loved someone—had taken Amy nearly three months. And it had been accompanied by a whole lot of denial and fear.

"What's funny?"

"Nothing."

It was true. Oh, *God*, it was true. The man who'd said sex with her had been unimportant and inconsequential…

No, he'd said the words but had been unsure if he'd chosen them correctly. She was ascribing meanings to him that weren't necessarily there. And he'd said he was glad she was here. That had to count for something, right?

Realizing he was still staring at her as if she had two heads, she tried to find a subject that was straightforward—that would conceal the huge shift that had just happened inside of her. "What is your mom cooking?"

"Feijoada."

"I thought it smelled familiar. My mom used to fix that on special occasions. It was a lot of work, but it was so, so good."

"Well, my mom has three great loves in this life. My dad, sewing and cooking. Not necessarily in that order."

She grinned, not so sure why she was suddenly feeling so giddy.

It was supposed to be a fling—a one-night stand. Not true love.

Maybe it wasn't. Maybe she was mistaken. It could be the country itself that she was in love with. As in she would love to stay here.

But she couldn't. Her life was back home.

So where did that leave them? Nowhere. She had no real idea how Roque even felt about her.

Taking her hand, he towed her into the living room. He was at ease in this environment. And as he introduced her to aunts and uncles and three or four cousins, she spotted something on a tall shelving unit in the corner. As Roque continued talking to his relatives, she tugged her hand free, making her way over to the case, where trophies and ribbons and newspaper articles were encased in ornate frames.

She read the name on a couple of the awards and realized these were Roque's. All of them. From his football days. In one framed photograph, a very young-looking Roque stood with Enzo Dos Santos, who introduced him as Chutegol's newest player.

She glanced at Roque to find him watching her. He didn't look quite so carefree anymore as he made his way toward her. And that hitch in his step was a constant reminder of what had changed in his life.

He grimaced. "She treats it like a shrine. Refuses to throw it out. Any of it."

Amy's eyes widened. "You don't seriously want her to, do you? This is part of your life history. Your journey to where you are now."

"It's not relevant anymore. I'm not a fan of hanging on to things that are in the past. Or of saying long goodbyes to things I can't retrieve. I'd rather the cut be swift and final."

The almost brutal words jogged something inside of her. She tried to connect them with something, but couldn't find where to put them.

Just then Roque's mom called them to the dinner table.

She sat next to the orthopedist while seven other people gathered around the meal. In front of them were long wooden trays loaded with different types of meat and sausages. Rice and beans were in deep, black cauldron-like bowls. There were orange slices and shredded sautéed greens. And it looked like home. Like her mom. She blinked moisture from her eyes.

"Andre isn't back, but that's the life of a *polícia*. He'll understand if we start without him."

Claudia stood and served everyone, rather

than passing bowls around the table like they might do in the States. When she got to Amy, she said, "Can I put a little of each on your plate, or is there something you don't like?"

"I think I will love all of it."

Including your son.

Soon they were all served and dug into their food. As she suspected, it was luscious and succulent and she was pretty sure she would have to waddle her way out of the house by the time it was all over. Claudia was a wonderful hostess, engaging everyone and making each person feel special.

Including Amy.

She'd half suspected the woman to try to matchmake or make a sideways comment, but she never did. She just smiled and kept everyone's plates and glasses filled.

Maybe it was the wine, but as she looked around the table, she was suddenly glad she'd gone to see her uncle, hoped someday she could meet her cousins as well and have a little of what Roque's family seemed to have. They were full of happiness and hope and just plain love of life.

When Claudia tried to fill her glass again, she shook her head. "Thank you, but I am very, very full. It was all so delicious."

"Mamãe, would you excuse us? I want to give Amy a tour of the house."

"Of course." His mom lifted her glass and smiled over the top of it. "I'll make sure to call you if your father comes home."

He showed her the grounds and the various rooms of the house, taking her up the stairs, showing her the guest bedrooms before walking into his childhood room. Once she was inside, he closed the door and leaned back against it while she looked around. Only in here there were no trophies or pictures of his various accomplishments in football. Instead, there were clippings of various medical cases he had helped with. Pictures of him graduating from medical school.

"*This* is my life. Not the football stuff. I want to live in the present, not cling to the past."

Amy turned to face him. He was speaking in riddles today, and she wasn't quite sure what any of it meant. But when he pushed away from the door and walked toward her, Amy's mouth went dry. He had the same look in his eye that he'd had the day they made love.

"Did I tell you how beautiful you look tonight?"

"No. But then I didn't tell you how handsome you look, either. But you do."

"I thought you didn't find me all that attractive."

"I lied."

He laughed, then reached for her hand and slowly reeled her in. "I've had a hard time taking my eyes off you all night."

Splaying her hands against his chest, she tipped her head back to look at that firm jaw, the slightest dusting of stubble across his chin making her want to slide her fingers across the scruff, let it tickle her cheek, her neck… Her lips parted as the thoughts continued.

"I didn't really want to give you a tour of the house, you know. I wanted to get you alone."

"You did?" She smiled. "I never would have guessed."

"I think that is yet another lie."

"Maybe." Happiness shimmered in her belly, making its rounds as it captured more and more of her doubts and locked them away. "Why did you want to get me alone?"

"So I could do this." His kiss took her by surprise. It wasn't the hard, desperate kisses from their night together. No, this was the slow brushing of lips. The touch and release that repeated over and over until she was breathless for more. He whispered her name, drawing it out in a low murmur that set her heart on fire, made her hope he actually felt something for her, despite what he'd told her in the courtyard at the hospital.

"I want to come to your house, after this. Say yes. Please." His hand came up and cupped her breast, thumb finding her nipple with a precision that made her breath catch. "Afterward I want to talk."

Talk. If his behavior right now was any indication of what he wanted to say to her, it couldn't be bad. Right? Because right now the man was burning red hot and setting her on fire right along with him.

"Yes. And I have something I want to tell you, too. I think I—"

A long pained scream from below shattered the intimacy in an instant.

"It's Mom."

He let her go and opened the door, hurrying down the stairs and leaving her to follow. When she got to the bottom Claudia was in Roque's arms sobbing uncontrollably, her choppy speech too broken up for her to follow.

And then Roque's eyes came up, and in them was a kind of pain she'd never seen before.

"My father has been shot."

CHAPTER ELEVEN

ROQUE DIDN'T CALL her like he'd said he would when he'd dropped her off at her house on his way to the hospital. And as the hours grew longer she became more and more concerned. She'd offered to go with him, but he thanked her and said he needed to be with his family right now, effectively shutting her out.

She didn't think he meant to; he was just in a hurry. Completely understandable. He was worried.

Well, so was she. She cared about his parents, too. Maybe more than she should.

And she'd been almost convinced he cared about her, too, after the way he talked to her in the bedroom.

She finally gave up waiting and tried to call his cell phone, but it went straight to voice mail after one ring. She didn't leave a message. There was no need. He would know what she wanted. She decided to just go up there instead. She could at least show him support, even if he had to stay by his father's bedside.

Or was it too late? Had he died, and they were all trying to come to terms with it? Seeing Claudia broken and weeping in her son's arms had torn her heart in two. She'd felt helpless, unsure what to do.

She still did.

And that look in Roque's eyes…

She saw it every time she blinked. The despair. The horror.

Calling a taxi, she went to the elevator, glancing at Lara's door and remembering the day of the party and how her eyes had widened when she saw Roque standing in the corridor with her. How embarrassed she'd been.

It seemed like forever ago. And now it was almost over. The goodbye party was rushing toward them at breakneck speed, and once that happened she would have one more day before she boarded a flight taking her back to the States.

And she hadn't told Roque how she felt. She'd started to in the bedroom just before he got the news about his father. And she certainly couldn't do it now.

The taxi ride took a mere ten minutes, but it seemed like hours. The closer they got, the more uneasy she became. If he'd wanted her there, he wouldn't have taken the time to drop her off at the house; he would have just gone straight to the hospital.

Unimportant. Inconsequential.

He'd never taken those words back.

Roque had been a star footballer. He was probably used to adulation and women throwing themselves at him.

Do you really think he could fall for someone like you?

The insecurities she'd felt when she first came to Brazil surfaced all over again: What did she think she was doing here?

But the taxi had pulled up outside of the hospital, so it was too late to turn around. So swallowing, she got out of the vehicle and paid the driver before slowly walking toward the entrance of the hospital.

She spotted Roque immediately; he was sitting in one of the chairs facing the glassed-in entrance to the emergency room, his head between his hands. No one else was around him.

Oh, God. Had his father died? He was a police officer, one of the most dangerous jobs in all of Brazil. She hesitated by the door, trying to decide whether or not she should intrude. Then his head came up and he speared her with a look. He looked neither angry nor glad. He just looked…empty.

She slowly made her way over, clasping her hands together. She sat, leaving one chair in between them, just in case he really didn't want her there.

He sucked in a deep breath and blew it out. "I saw that you called."

Amy had assumed he was busy with his father or trying to comfort his mother. But maybe he just hadn't wanted to talk to her. "I didn't leave a message. I figured you had other things to think about." She hesitated. "How is he?"

"He's in surgery. They don't know if he's going to make it or not." He swore softly. "He went into one of the *favelas* to make an arrest and there was a shootout. A bullet nicked his femoral artery. He almost bled out at the scene. His heart stopped on the ride over."

"I'm so sorry. Your mom...?"

He looked away. "She's in the chapel, praying."

And Roque was not. He was out here. Alone.

The people who were at the house were nowhere to be seen. Maybe they were in the chapel with his mom.

She wanted to touch his hand, but the space between them seemed too great, and not just in terms of physical space. There was something distant in his attitude. Maybe it was just fear and worry.

"What can I do?"

"Nothing. If he lives, he'll have a long recovery ahead of him. That has to take priority for me." He turned to look at her. "I've asked to be replaced for the rest of the lecture series, so you'll be working with someone else for the remainder of your stay. I probably won't be at the sendoff party. Or see you before you leave. I'm sorry about that."

He was sorry that he wouldn't be there to see her leave? But not about the fact that she *was* leaving? That he might never see her again?

She was being selfish. The man's father might die, for God's sake. She could always talk to him on the phone before she left.

And maybe it would go straight to voice mail like it had tonight.

What had he said back at the house?

His voice ran through her head as if he were reciting the words all over again: *"I'm not a fan of hanging on to things that are in the past. Or of saying long goodbyes to things I can't retrieve. I'd rather the cut be swift and final."*

He hadn't offered to keep her updated on how his dad was doing, while she was here or once she left Brazil.

Her stomach cramped with grief.

She wasn't going to sit by the phone and

wait, though. Not this time. Evidently ghosting could occur while the person was sitting right beside you.

She stood. "I understand. You need to be here with your dad. Please tell your mom that I'm thinking about her and hope Andre will be okay."

"Thank you."

Amy looked at him for a long time, committing the lines and planes of his face to memory. Then in a soft voice she said, "Goodbye, Roque."

And with that, she turned and walked away.

She was right. He didn't contact her—although she had heard that his father pulled through his surgery. Nor had he come to see the final days of Enzo's physical therapy treatments. And he was nowhere to be seen at the party, which was now in full swing.

These festivities didn't seem as new or full of hope as the welcome party had. Amy could see Francisco Carvalho chatting quietly to Krysta, his face full of sadness. And her friend told her that Flávia had been bitten by a venomous snake not long ago and had almost died. Thankfully she'd made an almost miraculous recovery. Amy hoped there were enough miracles floating around to touch Roque's dad in his long rehabilitation. She still wished Roque well. Despite a heart that was swollen and heavy. Of all the people to fall in love with.

All she could do was go home and do her best to forget him. Pack him away like that white eyelet dress of hers.

She could throw herself into her doctoral studies where she had no time to think about anything except school. Roque was right about one thing: letting go of the past. She'd held on to her parents' home for far too long, treating it almost like a shrine, the way Roque's mom did with his football memorabilia. She loved her mom and dad and they would always be with her, but she needed to make a fresh start. Maybe even in another part of the country.

This time she could do things right and not hold on to what she couldn't have. So, taking one last look around the swanky decor with its loud music and sad goodbyes, she looked for the nearest exit and showed herself out.

Roque's dad was finally out of the woods after three grueling weeks of advances and setbacks. He was going to have to go through cardiac rehab to strengthen the damaged muscle in his heart, and it would take months before he could go back to work, and that might not even happen if he couldn't recover enough of his strength. But he was nearing retirement age and was thinking about just handing in his badge and drawing his pension. It was certainly what his mom wanted.

And what did Roque want?

He knew he hadn't been exactly welcoming when Amy came to the hospital, but his thoughts had been so chaotic he hadn't had time to think. His dad's surgery had made him realize how uncertain life was. How painful endings could be. As he'd sat in the waiting room his thoughts had turned to Amy right about the time her call came through.

When Roque's own injury had sidelined him, he'd tried his damnedest to hold on to his old life, convincing himself that he was going to play football again. It had taken the reality of using a walker for months, and a visit from Enzo Dos Santos, to make him realize he needed to let go.

Which is what he'd needed to do with Amy. She had her whole life ahead of her. Her whole career. He told her he knew she was going to get her doctorate one day, and she said she was planning to start working on it when she got home. She couldn't do that if he was sitting there clinging to her, like he'd clung to his football dreams.

He'd had no business sleeping with her. Or anything else. It had been rash and irresponsible, and if he'd followed through with what he'd been about to tell her in his childhood bedroom, he could have derailed her life. It had been on the tip of his tongue to ask her to stay in Brazil. With him.

He realized as he was sitting at his mother's dinner table that he loved the woman.

In a way that he couldn't say of any other woman. Not even Halee.

And as his mom sat in the chapel of the hospital, begging her husband to stay with her, begging God to keep him there by any means necessary, he knew he couldn't do the same with Amy. He wasn't going to ask some deity to make her stay, wasn't going to make promises he couldn't keep.

He was going to let her go. *Because* he loved her. Because he wanted her life to be as rich and full as it could be. His life before his accident had been selfish and self-serving. He thought he'd grown past all of that. Until he realized he'd be going back to his old ways if he asked her to stay.

There was a knock at his office door. He grunted at whoever it was to come in, only to meet his mom's chiding face.

"Roquinho, is this how you greet your mother?"

"I'm sorry. Is Papai okay?"

"He is in rehab and doesn't want me there. He can't stand for me to see him weak. What he doesn't know is that he's the strongest man I've ever met." She leaned over his desk, her hands planted on its surface. "And I thought you were just like him. But now I am not so sure."

He barely kept himself from rolling his eyes. He knew exactly where she was headed with this. "She's going to continue her education, Mamãe. I'm not going to keep her from her dreams."

"Did you *ask* her what her dreams were?"

"I already know what they are."

"So you didn't. And when you were hiding in your bedroom with her? Why did you not ask her then?"

He couldn't hold back a laugh. "How did you know where we were?"

"I know where all young men want to go with a pretty woman. One they're in love with." She dropped into the chair in front of his desk. "Don't try to deny it."

He gritted his teeth and forced his way through. He did not want to talk right now. Not about Amy. Not about anything. He wanted to work.

"It changes nothing."

She leaned forward. "Why not ask her?"

"I already told you. I know what she

wants." He picked up a pencil and twirled it between his fingers. "Asking her to give that up would be selfish."

"Why would you ask her to give it up? A...what did you say? Doctorate? It takes how long to get?"

"I don't know. Three years. Why?"

She blinked. "Oh, Roquinho. Don't you see? Three years is not such a long time."

"I don't see how any of this—"

She held up her hand. "She left Brazil to pursue her dream, yes? So why can you not leave Brazil...to pursue *her*?"

He sat back in his chair, the creaky wheels in his head starting to turn again. For someone who was not even a surgeon, his mom had cut clean through to the heart of the matter. Why couldn't he go to the States to be with her, while she worked on her degree? With his credentials, he could probably do something while he was there, maybe even research how to get his certification in the States. But that wasn't what was important; it was something that could be decided afterward. Once they both got what they wanted: Amy her degree and a fulfilling career. And maybe Roque…could somehow, in some weird twist of the universe, get Amy.

If she would even have him after the way he'd brushed her off.

All he could do was try. The question was, was he willing to?

Yes.

He came around the desk and took his mom's wise face in his hands, giving her a hard kiss on the cheek. "Have I ever told you how glad I am that you're my mother?"

"I think you just did."

She stood up and hugged him tightly. When she let him go, he saw tears in her eyes.

"Now, go. And tell her I would like to work on another of her dresses. This time it will be white with layers and layers of lace."

"I'll tell her. I promise."

CHAPTER TWELVE

AMY SAT IN her first day of classes, trying to concentrate on what the professor was saying. But even two months post-Roque, her thoughts still returned toward him. And it made her furious.

He doesn't love you, Amy. Get over it.

He would have made some effort to contact her if he felt anything at all. She'd been so, so sure that he cared when he kissed her that last time in his bedroom. But she'd given him every opportunity to say something. And instead there was only silence. A silence which continued even now.

Class was dismissed, and she headed out to the parking lot, slinging her book bag over her shoulder. Getting her degree seemed so worthless right now. *Right now* being the operative words. Once she stopped daydreaming about a certain Brazilian orthopedic surgeon and stopped seeing him at every turn, like at that lamppost over there.

She rolled her eyes, until she realized she'd never actually seen him teleported from her head to a physical location. Looking again, thinking she'd just mistaken someone else for him, she stopped dead in her tracks when she realized she wasn't mistaken. And he hadn't teleported.

He was here. In Florida, looking just as outrageously gorgeous as he had in Brazil.

Then he smiled. And, just like always, something inside of her somersaulted.

What was he doing here? Was he at a conference?

Maybe—but that didn't answer the question. Why was he *here*? At the university where she just happened to be studying.

He pushed away from the post and walked toward her, his cane nowhere to be seen.

"Is…is your dad okay?"

"He's still in rehab. And retiring from the force, which makes my mother very happy."

"I'm so glad." And she was. She knew Andre had survived his surgery, but the last news she'd heard after that was that it was still touch and go.

She had been in contact with Krysta and Flávia, and it seemed she wasn't the only one who'd had man trouble while in Brazil. She'd been too busy with her own love life to realize that her two friends were also sliding down the same slippery slope she'd been stuck on.

She hoped they both got their happy endings, but as for her, she'd been so sure she wouldn't be one of them...

Except Roque was here.

"Let's try that again, shall we?" The smile was still in place. "Hello, Amy."

"Hi."

Good going—you couldn't think of anything more profound than that?

"You look good. You've started on your studies obviously." He nodded at her bag.

"I have." Why wasn't he telling her why

he was here? Was he trying to torture her? Had she left something behind in Brazil?

Ha! She had. But it wasn't something you could pack in a bag and carry through customs.

"Can we walk?" The last word stuck in her throat. She remembered the last time she'd suggested they do that. It had been to say that sleeping together had been a mistake. And it evidently had been. But try as she might, she couldn't make herself regret the short amount of time they'd spent together. She'd hold it with her for the rest of her life, just like that shrine Roque's mom had made out of his football artifacts. Because he was wrong. Some things shouldn't be tossed away as if they never existed.

He fell into step beside her, that little hitch of his still in evidence. But she loved it. Still loved everything about him.

"I don't know where to start. Other than to say I was wrong."

"Wrong?"

"Wrong to not call you. Wrong to not try

to work out some kind of alternate solution for a very real problem."

She stopped, her heart flipping around in her chest. "What problem is that?"

"The fact that I live in Brazil, and you live in Florida." He smiled. "It took my mom to make me realize that it's not such a big problem at all."

Was he kidding? This wasn't just a matter of physical distance. He'd been like a water spigot. On one second and off the next.

"But you were hot, then cold, and now... I'm very confused." Her mind was still stuck somewhere behind her and was pedaling as fast as it could to catch up. "I thought you weren't a fan of long goodbyes."

"I'm not. But I was mistaken in thinking this had to be goodbye at all."

And just like that, the spigot was on again. She wasn't sure she'd be able to survive if he suddenly turned it back off. She needed to be sure. Very sure.

"Are you saying you don't want it to be?"

His fingers bracketed her face, and her eyes shut at the exquisiteness of feeling his skin on hers once again. "No. I don't want it to be."

"But how can you be sure? You were so distant at the hospital."

He gave a pained laugh. "Part of it was the shock of the shooting, but part of it was the realization that your future was half a world away from mine. I was trying to do the right thing and let you walk out of my life."

"Try? You were very good at it, from what I remember."

"I know. And you don't know how many times I've regretted it. Am I too late?"

No, he wasn't. And hearing his explanation made all the missing pieces fall into place. She finally understood why he'd seemed so distant. So completely unmoved by her presence. She'd done quite a bit of pretending herself over the course of her time in Brazil. Suddenly she knew what she was going to do. He'd sacrificed something. Maybe it was time for her to do the same.

"I can drop out of the program. I only just started and—"

"No. You're not going to do that. I want you to finish."

She reveled in his words, his touch…his very presence. In those talented hands that were bringing hope back to life. "I don't want you to feel you have to wait for me, though."

"My grasp of English is not always good, but I think if we change out one little word, it will make more sense. I'm not going to wait *for* you, Amy. I'm going to wait *with* you. Here in Florida." He stopped for a second. "I love you. I was wrong not to say the words earlier, to let you go the way I did. Once I realized the truth, there was still my visa to get and flights to be arranged. What I had to say couldn't be said over the phone, which is why I didn't call you."

He kissed her cheek. "I'm hoping maybe you feel a little something for me, too."

There were a couple more things she needed to understand, although she was pretty sure she already knew the answers.

"You called our time together unimportant."

"Yes. I knew that I'd chosen the wrong word. Because it wasn't unimportant. It turned out to be the most important thing I'd ever done in my life. More important than my football days. More important than my medical career. I found love, when I thought I never would again."

She shut her eyes, and when she reopened them, he was still there, the imprint of his lips still fresh on her face. "You crazy, gorgeous surgeon, I do love you. You had to realize."

"I thought I had. But when my dad was shot, I realized I didn't want you giving everything up for me. But you don't have to."

She thought for a moment. But that still left… "I don't want you giving everything up for me, either."

"That is a bridge we can cross in three years. When you walk down the aisle of the university and hold your degree in your hands."

He was really going to do it. He was moving here. For her. Because of her. With her. There were all kinds of prepositions she could substitute that would each end with her being with the man she loved.

"Paulista let you leave?"

"They did not have a choice. I was coming, whether they liked it or not. But the administrator assured me that I would have a job waiting if I ever decided to come back."

If he ever. "You mean you might stay here? For good?"

"It's a possibility. I actually contacted a nearby hospital and asked what the process would be to have my medical license transferred over. They want me to come in for talks. But I didn't want to commit unless I know where your heart is."

"That's the easiest question of all, Roque. My heart is wherever you are. I love you."

He leaned over and kissed her, this time on the lips, right there in the parking lot of the university. The world around them was still turning, but she felt like this moment was suspended in time. When he finally raised his head, he said, "Before I forget. My mom has a message for you."

"She does?"

"She wants you to know that she has dreams of her own. Of working on another of your dresses. Only this one would be all white and would see me waiting for you at the end of another kind of aisle."

He reached in his pocket and fished out a little velvet container. But when he started to go down on one knee, she stopped him. "Your leg."

"My leg will survive. Let me do this." He knelt in front of her and snapped open the lid of the box. Inside was a gorgeous ring, a center diamond flanked by two glowing emeralds. "Amy Woodell, will you marry me? Both here and in Brazil?"

"Yes. Oh, yes! I'll marry you wherever you want."

"We can have the ring resized, but I wanted to bring it." He plucked it from its velvet bed and slid it onto her finger. It fit almost perfectly. "I love it." She couldn't stop looking at it, almost too afraid to believe this was happening.

"Amy?"

"Yes?" She shifted her attention back where he was still kneeling in front of her.

"When you're done admiring that, I may have overestimated the abilities of my leg."

She stared at him, then realized what he meant and burst out laughing. Laughter she tried her best to suppress. It was no good.

In between chuckles, she managed to get out, "Here. Let me help."

She hauled him to his feet, and soon all thoughts of laughter were swept away by the power of Roque's kiss.

And by the very strength of his love.

EPILOGUE

AMY WAS NOT the bride. Not this time, anyway.

That had happened six months earlier, and Claudia had indeed made her dress.

But she *was* one of the bridesmaids at this particular ceremony, as was Flávia. Her two lecture series friends had also gotten their happy endings, and she was thrilled for them both.

Krysta and Francisco stood in an intimate circle of their family and closest friends and repeated the vows they'd written to each other, their voices ringing with happiness and conviction.

Roque gripped her hand tightly, leaning slightly on his cane today. But it was okay. They'd each learned to provide support to the other when it was needed the most.

Krysta's wedding was much different from her own, but it was still beautiful, their love for each other permeating the air around them.

She glanced to her right and caught sight of Flávia holding her baby against her chest, her husband's arm around her shoulders. No one had realized the venom specialist was pregnant during the last part of their stay in Brazil, not even the man standing next to her.

Those days spent together at Paulista seemed like an eternity ago. But the hospital's pull on them was still strong, the bonds forged during their time together proving to be unbreakable. Unlike Roque's words, she didn't want to say goodbye to that past, since it had played a role in the future they were carving out together.

And whether they decided to come back to Brazil after she earned her degree or stay in the States, she knew it wouldn't matter one way or the other as long as they were together.

Evidently the other two couples felt the same way, because standing in a simple garden in a small Brazilian town near where Francisco's family lived, the friends were bearing witness to a love they'd all found.

The officiating minister lifted his right hand and pronounced Krysta and Francisco husband and wife. And when he invited the bride and groom to kiss, it wasn't the only kiss that was had in that tiny garden.

And it wouldn't be the only kiss in the days to come. For Brazil had woven a tapestry of love and friendship in their lives that would endure long after they said their goodbyes and left for different parts of the world.

Because that was what love did.

It endured. For always.

* * * * *